The Cape Breton Collection

Edited by Lesley Choyce

Pottersfield Press
Porters Lake, Nova Scotia, Canada

Canadian Cataloguing in Publication Data

Main entry under title:
The Cape Breton Collection

ISBN 0-919001-15-7

1. Canadian fiction (English) - Nova Scotia - Cape Breton Island. * 2. Canadian fiction (English) - 20th century.* 3. Canadian poetry (English) - Nova Scotia - Cape Breton Island.* 4. Canadian poetry (English) - 20th century* I. Choyce, Lesley, 1951 -

PS8255.C36C36 1983   C810'.8'097169   C83-098914-5

Acknowledgements:
"Wakeup Coaltown" by Jeremy Akerman is published by permission of the author.
Russell Buker's poems originally appeared in **The Antigonish Review** and are published by permission of the author.
"Snapshot: The Third Drunk" originally appeared in **The Atlantic Monthly** and is published by permission of the author.
"Lauchie and Lisa and Rory" originally appeared in **The Antigonish Review** and is published by permission of the author.
Don Domanski's poems originally appeared in books published by House of Anansi and appear here by the permission of the author.
"Stan Goes to the Doctor's" by Clive Doucet is published by permission of the author.
"The Feast of Christ the King" originally appeared in **The Pottersfield Portfolio** and is published by permission of the author.
Rita Joe's poems are published by permission of the author.
"Junk" by John E.C. MacDonald originally appeared in **The Pottersfield Portfolio** and is published by permission of the author.
Each Man's Son was originally published by MacMillan in 1951. Chapter 2 appears here by permission of the author.
"The Tuning of Perfection" by Alistair MacLeod is published by permission of the author.
R.J. MacSween's poems originally appeared in books published by The Antigonish Press and are published by permission of the author.
"Snow" by Farley Mowat appeared in **The Snow Walker** (McClelland and Stewart) and is published by permission of the author.
"Cranberry Head" by Ellison Robertson is published by permission of the author.
"The Dwarf in His Valley Ate Codfish" by Ray Smith originally appeared in **Cape Breton is the Thought Control Centre of Canada** (Anansi) and is published by permission of the author.

Photographs courtesy of the Nova Scotia
Department of Government Services, Information Division.

Published with the assistance of the Nova Scotia Department of Culture, Recreation, and Fitness.

Copyright 1984,1989 Pottersfield Press

Reprint   assistance provided by The Canada Council

Contents

Introduction		4
Wakeup Coaltown	Jeremy Akerman	8
Poetry	Russell Buker	28
Snapshot: The Third Drunk	Silver Donald Cameron	32
Lauchie and Lisa and Rory	Sheldon Currie	45
Poetry	Don Domanski	51
Stan Goes to the Doctor	Clive Doucet	56
The Feast of Christ the King	Donna Doyle	63
Poetry	Rita Joe	67
Junk	John E.C. MacDonald	72
Each Man's Son: Chapter 2	Hugh MacLennan	82
The Tuning of Perfection	Alistair MacLeod	93
Poetry	R.S. MacSween	122
Snow	Farley Mowat	126
Cranberry Head	Ellison Robertson	134
The Dwarf in his Valley	Ray Smith	152

Introduction

In 1820, Cape Breton was annexed to the province of Nova Scotia. Not long after, the industrialized world caught up with the island. The mines opened up with coal to power the machinery of progress and in 1900 a steel plant was built in Sydney. Cape Breton had always been a rugged place but this was something different. The independent hard work of hauling nets or plowing rocky soil was translated for many into the backbreaking labour of digging out the coal and forging the steel for the company.

Islanders needed work and they needed money but when they jumped in with two bootheels cracking down into the middle of the twentieth century, they paid the inevitable price of development. But along with industry came unions and a breed of radicalism unheard of in the Maritimes. The coal miners' strike of 1925 remains one of the longest and most bitter on record. And when the times were desperately hard in the 1920s, miners were forced to look for outside help, accepting the generosity of the Quaker Oats Company but turning down the support of Lenin's Soviet government. In the end, Cape Bretoners had to look out for themselves, and through some inbred sense of dogged perseverance, they survived.

The literature of Cape Breton displays epic struggles between men and the sea, men and industry, men and money, men and government and even men against their own ancestral spirit. It is an island of conflict. And yet the first thought that strikes you when you drive onto the island, across the Causeway and beyond the thin suburban veneer that hugs the Canso Strait, is this: it is one of the most beautiful islands to be found anywhere.

The Cape Breton Collection is an anthology of fiction and poetry written by Cape Bretoners in the last forty years . When Hugh MacLennan published *Each Man's Son* in 1951 he published a book about "Everyman" but also a work that emerges from his own love for Cape Breton. "Continents are much alike," he writes in the prologue to the novel, "and a man can no more love a continent than he can love a hundred million people. But all the islands of the world are different. They are small enough to be known, they are vulnerable, and men come to feel about them as they do about women."

As you read through the brief biographies here you'll see a curious mix of Cape Bretoners who have left and Cape Bretoners who have arrived. Ray Smith of Mabou writes from Montreal, "I never forget that I was a little boy in paradise . . . and maybe if I work hard and live a good life, and if I'm lucky . . . then perhaps I'll get to live in paradise again some day." And Farley Mowat, born in Ontario and well travelled in parts civilized and otherwise, has come to settle near River Bourgeois. Of Cape Breton, he says, "I think so much of it that I've chosen to live there over any other place on earth I've ever seen."

In this collection I have assembled writings that emphasize the human side of Cape Breton: the music, the families, the religion, the language, and the cultural depths. You will also find the fist fights, the drinking, the decay and the despair. If you like, think of this as a tour book, a tourist's guide, the kind that doesn't point out curious cairns or outcroppings or quaint churches, but one that directs you into the kitchens, the gardens, the taverns, the junkyards, and the soul of Cape Breton.

As Alistair MacLeod asserts, music plays a vital part in the life of the people here; dramatically so. My private vision of Cape Breton is the memory of sitting at sunset on the front porch of an old farmhouse in Deepdale, outside of Inverness. A fine mist was settling in the valley below where two neighbors were playing fiddle and bagpipes for their own enjoyment. The beauty, the calm and the music welded a tiny private euphoria inside me that can never be removed.

The corollary to that moment was a Sunday morning in March about eight years later. I was walking alone down a road near Gardiner Mines. A blizzard from the northeast that had closed the Causeway to mainlanders was hammering snow, ice and bitter wind across a grey land while I stared at the unbent arrogance of the Lingan power plant stack. I passed a house with an open second story window and inside a rock band was practising a potent, screeching Cape Breton blues. I felt that I had arrived at the loneliest place I had ever known.

I have not included the great songwriters of Cape Breton in the anthology only because I fear that to publish their lyrics and rob them of their music would not do them justice. Suffice it to say that music is such an important part of the life here that the struggle to endure might have ended in defeat without it. I will let Alistair MacLeod say the rest in *"The Tuning of Perfection."*

Assembled are fifteen gifted writers, some of them major figures of Canadian literature, all having shared an island fertile to imaginative development, a vortex for private conflicts, passions and possibilities. There are full fledged novelists, teachers, and professors of literature, well-praised poets and hard-hitting journalists. You will also find a critically acclaimed painter, two men of government, a MicMac mother of eight, a housewife returned to a family homestead, a railroad man, a priest, and a self-sufficient farmer. Their words are the modern legends of Cape Breton.

In 1983, a staunch group of Cape Breton farmers and landowners lost a court battle to stop a multi-national forestry corporation from spraying toxic herbicides on Cape Breton forests.

After losing in the courts, they stood to lose their own homes in settlement to their opponent. Their defeat, however, was not met with pessimism but persistence. Once again, support came in from across North America and around the world.

It's a little bit like the early strikes by hard-pressed Cape Breton coal miners. The willingness to carry on in the face of defeat is somehow intrinsic to the nature of the Cape Breton spirit. The land of the Goliath, Angus (Giant)MacAskill, is also the land of David and Goliath battles.The literature of Cape Breton is a compendium of fighters, of winners and losers, but most of all, survivors.

Lesley Choyce
January 1, 1984

Jeremy Akerman / Glace Bay

Jeremy Akerman was born in the United Kingdom in 1942. He immigrated to Canada in the 1960's and worked as an archaeologist, a reporter and a radio announcer. Chosen as provincial leader of the New Democratic Party in 1968, he was elected to the Legislature to represent his home riding of Glace Bay in 1970. Akerman now serves on the Policy Board of the Nova Scotia government.

Along with writing newspaper and magazine articles, Akerman has written and directed plays for theatre companies in Nova Scotia. Two non-fiction books, **What Have You Done for Me Lately?** and **Jeremy Akerman's Cookbook** appeared in 1977. **Black Around the Eyes,** an historical novel concerning Cape Breton coal miners ,was published in 1981. "Wakeup Coaltown" is a shortened version of a longer work and it appears in print here for the first time.

Wake Up Coaltown

by Jeremy Akerman

The great, grey, half-wild cat which Dinny Morrison calls "the christly stonky beast" pauses before the tatty old pair of boots, one front paw poised in the crisp air. The other quivers with caution from the ugly, bloody battle scarred shoulder down to the muddy toes which are twitching in the thin, brittle white covering on the bottom of the ditch. It is the first frost of the season and the beast's eyes are bright, the ends of its ragged fur pointed and stiff and its wet, dripping nostrils blowing steamy white clouds.

The boots, which are not properly laced, are attached to a spindly pair of legs encased in filthy, worn and, in places, paper thin jeans which long ago surrendered any claim to being called blue, as the mud of the ditch, the grime of the dock, the coal dust of the yard and the spillings of a thousand beers have brought them to the point where "dirt coloured" is the only accurate description. Not so the scarlet mackinaw which, hanging open amidships, reveals a once white belly now blackened in every pore and matter by pale ginger hair. This tartan beauty was liberated last night from a peg in the smoky, heaving tavern and was borne like the cold east wind through the reeling town, up the staggering hill and to this very ditch where its virgin wool was savagely ravished as its bearer crashed headlong through the alder bush and into the muck. Protruding from within the collar of this newly won trophy is the grimy, leathery neck and the devastated and fuddled head of the Poet.

Lemuel Kelly has always been called the Poet. He was called that long before he met his match in the two gentlemen he describes as the Captain and the Governor (Morgan and General respectively) because in school he had always dazzled the class with recitations of Milton and Dryden (garbled snatches of which he still declaims either to impress priests that he is going straight or to debase himself for the entertainment of those who might, in return, give him the price of a pint) and the second page of the yearbook had always been reserved for Lem's own flowery verses commemorating the achievements of the school or lauding the dignity of coal mining.

The Poet receives an honorarium in the amount of fifteen dollars per week from the County welfare office in recognition of his services to literature and when, as is always the case within one day, the money is gone, he goes on the bum with his bleary eyed cronies shuffling on from drink to drink, fouling and obstructing the streets of the town by the sea. Nobody knows when the Poet last had a square meal, it is not something he talks about.

Above the ditch, out of sight of the cat, the belt of cloud low lying over the end of the ocean starts to lighten on its under edges and the black pithead suddenly appears out of the gloom. Between the tiny crack separating the black sea and the ash grey cloud a delicate streak of pure gold pencils itself across the sky. A minute flicker breaks the perfection of the golden line, momentarily catching the leaves of the alder. The cat lets its paw drop to the ground as it looks up and through the branches. The flicker becomes a small burst of fire which speeds across the ocean, flashes over the land and stabs at Raines Hill, creeping over the edge of the ditch and startling the cat. The fire gleams in its eyes and with a sniff it steps on to the Poet's chest and prepares to leap up the bank. At that moment another needle of gold flashes directly into the ditch and full into the Poet's ravaged face. The black slits jump open, then widen, as his right arm jerks up at the animal, sending it sprawling and screeching.

"Frig off, you jeesly bastard!" The Poet utters his opening lines to a new day.

The Poet's face has nothing if it lacks character. It actually belongs to a man of forty-six, but it looks as if it has seen at least sixty winters. The hair is long and unkempt, caked with mud at the back, and curling over and into the dirt clogged ears. The lines around the eye slits are etched deep and are accentuated by the deposits within them. The lips are dry and cracked. The nose is long with pinched nostrils from which emerge scraggy hairs matted and stiff with frozen mucous. A large, black bruise adorns the Poet's left cheek, four deep scratches his right, and a deep, festering cut his furrowed brow. Some weeks since the Poet attempted to shave, haltingly, unevenly, finally abandoning the effort, the thick stubble and the dark red scabs marking the battleground of his encounter with the unsteady razor. As the gold now overflows into the ditch, the Poet blinks again and breathes heavily, baring his yellow and rotting teeth in the process and releasing a cloud of frosty stale liquor-ridden breath.

Away to his right sits the cat, suspiciously regarding him out of the corner of its eye, then the road, white and as yet unmarked by any tire, the row of houses, the church of the Sacred Heart, the jumble of crisp pink and grey rooftops, the cold and stiff boats at the quay, and Gillis' warehouse where Neilie the Wharf Rat will soon be brewing tea on a little Coleman stove. The Poet cogitates as he blinks into the sun, now a quarter up and blinding the landscape with glory. Neilie's hot tea sneaks into his mind like a lost love or a forgotten errand. It will not be as good as the Governor, but it will be wet, and Neilie's little corner will be warm and there may be some makings for a smoke. Dragging himself out onto the road and pulling the mackinaw around him, Lem spits at the cat and raises his head into the brisk breeze which is carrying the salt from the sea. Behind the black slits, their sockets puffy and bruised, there still lurks intelligent life and it has made a decision. Slowly one boot slides in front of its mate and he begins a jerky trudge away down hill. The Poet is on the move; it is a signal for the town to wake up.

"Look at that stunned bastard," mutters 'Popeye' MacDougall as he strains his soapy neck towards the window to watch the Poet shamble past. "It's a frigging wonder he's still alive. Probably been out all night."

"What are you talking about Garfield?" asks Marion, his Jeckyll and Hyde wife, who, after sparking, flirting, and dancing up one hell of a Hydish storm at the legion last night, is now very Jeckyllish in her drab and stained nightie. Her hair is straggled and mousy without its aerosol glitter, her shoulders sloping like ski runs, her face pasty and drawn, the tantalising and voluptuous body which drew last night's whistles and held last night's stares now limp and childish.

Popeye takes a quick look at her over his shoulder then looks back. Oh Jesus, he sighs to himself, and his whole married life flashes before his eyes. If only Haddie Baker could see her now he wouldn't be wanting to dance six waltzes in a row, and Walter Debison would think twice about his nudges and winks and little laughs about going to Bermuda.

"Jesus Christ!" Popeye shouts at his razor, hurling it into the sink and into the faces of Haddie Baker and Walter Debison, "What the hell am I doing? I must still be drunk or something."

"What's wrong, Garfield?"

"Am I shaving to go into the pit, for Chrissakes?"

"Well, it don't matter when you shave."

"I always shave at nights," Popeye says wrathfully, "I never shave in the mornings unless its vacation. What the fuck is going on anyway these days? It's no good, Marion, this getting loaded at the Legion of a week night. I scarce know what I'm doing in the pit during the day."

"I didn't hear you complaining too much last night when you was telling jokes with Joe Priest and Tank Murphy and showing off to Millie MacLeod how fast you could drink a pint of beer."

"Well, at least I wasn't leaping about like a whore, sticking my tits in peoples' faces," Popeye buries his face in the big rough towel and mumbles from its safety, "and that ain't easy when you got to strap them up and bring your neckline down to your belly."

The slamming of the bedroom door alerts Popeye to the fact that his near and dear does not intend to continue the conversation and that he has to get his own tea. No time to lose, too, Joe Priest MacLennan will be expecting to be picked up in less than half an hour.

Joe Priest, this gleaming frosty morning, has ideas other than trumpfing down the coal mine to hack for black diamonds. Still a little hungover from last night's exertions, Joe is nonetheless in mellow friendly form and is fully occupied in trying to keep his slippery wife, Freda, still long enough to exercise his conjugal rights. Flouncy, buxom, yellow-haired Freda smells as generous as she feels, warm, full and inviting like a bakery. Her ample topography is fatally swaddled in the sheerest and silkiest of pale cream nightgowns which, having first set Joe Priest's rough hands delicately a-twitching, is now turning him into a king of the jungle, roaring, rampant and impatient as the frantically screaming kettle next door in Gordie Johnson's kitchen.

"Keep still for Jesus sake, will you!" Joe pants roughly.

"Hand off, you great fool," Freda replies, thrashing out at the invading forces, "you've got to go to your work. Popeye will be at the door in minutes."

"Frig!" Joe Priest throws back the bedclothes in disgust, making sure to expose his unrelenting wife to as much cold air as possible, and, with a rueful glance at what he considers to be a terrible waste, hobbles uncomfortably across the room and clatters down the stairs of their little company house.

Sitting quietly in front of his steaming tea, Gordie Johnson hears Joe leave. Late at night and early in the morning Gordie Johnson hears the whole world dashing, chasing, feeding, sleeping, breathing, ticking over. He has been unable to sleep for nearly fifteen years. Fifteen years ago he retired, and a month after he left the coal company's employ, Betty upped and died on him. At the Pensioners' Union club rooms, Gordie is the life and soul of merriment and horseplay, but here, at home, he is quiet, sad, and still his long, furrowed horselike face solemn and thoughtful, his bright yellow nicotine-stained fingers just touching the edge of the hot teacup. Gordie seldom wears his teeth and so his mouth almost disappears between the great long hooked nose and the huge jutting chin. When he sups his tea and takes a drag from his home-rolled cigarette his hollow cheeks almost touch in the middle. As he puffs and slurps in the little green oilskinned kitchen, Gordie, like the ancient brown clock on the mantle, is ticking away, killing time until the Pensioners' Club opens and, beyond that, until Betty calls him to join her.

The long low belt of grey cloud is starting to lift now and the world is gradually lightening as the golden line becomes a swath of brilliance. From the top of the Dump, where Willie Ross is struggling into his pit boots and listening to his old father snoring like a locomotive above his head, the town is being picked out, house by house, church by church, street by winding street in the spreading light as it rolls inexorably forward pushing last night's boozy, sleepy shadows up the hill and into the woods where they will lurk in damp, shrouded hollows until tonight calls them out again. Willie Ross is the only member of the household awake, something he bitterly resents. He aims a kick at the dog which is far too agile for him, gathers his work clothes and lunch can under his arm and stomps out into the back yard where his gleaming monster LTD - his pride though not his joy at month's end when the payment is due - slinks majestically in the brittle newborn sunshine.

Willie looks at his watch - too early as usual - surveys the yard with its rickety, but newly painted picket fence, ancient outdoor toilet which his father still insists on using even though Willie had installed a spanking modern bathroom facility when he became master of the house, the pile of old tires stacked against the wall, a heap of dog's droppings and, leading from them to - and over - the door of the car, a line of dirty yellow spots in the white front.

"Frigging dog," Willie mutters savagely; the sharp air pricks his lungs. The New Waterford Pages of the Cape Breton Post are flapping around the wheel of his car so Willie grabs them, stiff and crinkly, to wipe the urine from the door; it smears into an obscene yellowish-grey whorl on the white paintwork. With another quick glance at his watch, Willie turns about and looks out to sea. The golden band has widened now but has become paler, almost silver at the edges where it brushes against and thrusts up into the cloud, now no longer a solid grey belt, but breaking into separate swirls and puffs of cream and white and pale blue. Only at the very sea's end is there a golden spill on the water; across the vast expanse of dark grey-green ocean it is the silver which has picked out and flicked the tops of a million tiny waves all chopping and scrambling to get to shore.

As Willie's monster purrs out of the yard and down the rickety row towards the colliery, the other three occupants of the company house are fast asleep and wrapped in dreams. Annie, his miniature, neat, doll-like wife, each curl of her glossy black hair in place and her skin shining like a china tea plate, is in a Pampers commercial - in full colour, but with the edges of the picture blurred and hazy - floating in slow motion through a summer graden, gracefully bending to scoop a naked pink baby from a blanket and holding the dear little thing aloft, magically turning to the camera with a movement that swirls her pretty airy, flimsy dress up and around and out at the butterflies and birds, revealing a split second's worth of perfect smooth white thigh. Annie was never too interested in babies until Dr. Singh had told her she could not have one. Now she not only dreams of cute little girls with yellow curls and pink flounce dresses and glowing little boys in fluffy sleepers, but she clips out pictures of them from magazines and stores them, for her personal perusal only, in the big recipe book her cousin had given her when she and Willie were married. Willie, at first puzzled and then irritated by this fixation, has suggested time and again that they adopt a child, but Annie says it wouldn't be the same.

The next room sounds like Grand Central Station in the rush hour. Her mother-in-law, Marg, lies silent and undisturbed next to her roaring and raging husband as he rattles the window panes. After fifty years of marriage, old Marg simply does not hear a thing; the trumpeting elephant at her side could rouse the entire world, but she sleeps on oblivious, her little plump bosom scarcely moving and her gentle breath so slight and quiet that it does not even disturb the tiny white hairs on her red chin. She is not in Grand Central Station this early morning, but in the wandering valley of the Margaree standing outside her uncle's barn looking over the top of the pony trap to the apple trees in the steep orchard and the lush green fields which slide down to the peaceful river. She is eight years old again and is on a visit to the country with her starch-stiff, black garbed, pious parents who call each other "Mr." and "Mrs.", go to church three times on Sunday, and do not approve of picture books, dancing and boys. While her mother and father delicately and disdainfully pick their way through the dung spattered farm yard - not a speck finding its way onto their squeaky, gleaming shoes - and sit down to tea and biscuits in the dark and life smelling kitchen, little Marg is taking a slightly wrinkled but rosy and pungent apple from the shelf in the shed and, polishing it on her cotton dress, skips out into the sunlight among the silly red chickens, funny brown ducks and belligerent white geese.

A few inches away from her lies Diamond Donnie Ross, puffing and snorting like the 7:55 express to Montreal, his round belly a vast boiler of activity, his sagging red mouth the open firebox, his quivering nose the main valve, his tense limbs the stout rods straining to turn the great driving wheels forward. Although the 7:55 thunders and roars in the little bedroom with its shiny linoleum floors, flowery walls, and Woolco furniture, Diamond Donnie, in his innermost guarded, sacred and secret dreamnest, is also far away in the country of his youth. After more than half a turbulent century of footloose battling, boozing and brawling, Donnie Ross' dreams are carried time and again back to the gentle summer waters of the Bras D'or where, as a young man of twenty-three, he wandered hand in hand with his first, only real and lost love. It is the soft June evenings, when the warm breezes rustles the birch trees, which cause him the most pain, but even in the crisp fall days and the hard winter nights he is never immune from her haunting face, sweet breath, silken hands and supple body. At eighty-two, Diamond Donnie is still hale, boisterous and crusty and the one chink in his armour is unknown to anyone else in the world. As Jeanette's tender arms envelop him, her beautiful warm breasts press against him, and he lowers her onto the mossy bank beneath the tall elm, the 7:55 suddenly stops shunting, lets out a burst of steam and Donnie's eyes spring open to the new day. At the sound of silence Marg wakes.

"Another day," she raises herself and strains to see out of the window, "a dandy too by the looks of it."

"Cool though."

"Get some tea into yourself and you'll be alright."

"Sure," he says, still cranky, but gradually thawing, "and an egg or two wouldn't kill me."

"One maybe," Marg says cautiously, "got to watch the cholesterol."

"Jesus, Murphy and Joseph!" Donnie sits bolt upright in the bed and turns his wrathful eye full on her. "A few years and I'll be in Raines Road cemetery anyway and you're here fretting about an extra egg. God save us if we can't have a little pleasure out of life before we leave it. Pretty soon you'll be after nagging me again to quit smoking."

"Wouldn't do no harm," Marg says, wrinkling her little red nose, "dirty, filthy habit, stinking the place out."

"Well, just forget all about any ideas on that subject. You're going to have to put up with me the way I am for the next going off here, whether you like it or not," Donnie says, starting to smile, "and enough of this pecking and down to make my breakfast."

"Lord that's in a hurry today. Is the queen coming to town?"

"I've got to see Buck about a bit of business for the Pensioners Union."

"Pensioners Union! If you ask me that's what's an excuse to

smoke and play cards and tell yarns with the old lads, that's all, Business indeed!" She scoffs, swinging her feet down onto the floor, "and as for that Buck MacPhee, knowing him, the lazy devil, you won't be seeing him before noon I can tell you."

She is right. Portly, handsome, bald-headed Buck MacPhee and his ancient, beautiful wife May are sleeping peacefully and happily and have no intention of stirring until the sun is well over the hill. In their tiny, snug and spotless senior citizens unit on the Glory Hole slope, the MacPhees are thoroughly but lazily enjoying to the full the quiet contentment of retired life and watching each other grow older and lovelier with the passing days.

Down the slope, about a hundred yards away from the serenely snoozing MacPhees is a small black house with bright eggshell blue trim around its doors and windows. Its backyard has been scooped out of the hillside so that the house stands on a platform and leans into the slope as if preparing itself for a landslide which one day soon will bring crashing down upon its roof the senior citizens units and the coal seams upon which they are built. Inside the house are two people; Alfred Petrie, retired coal miner and his grown up but not yet, alas, married daughter, June, who is the precious bane of his existence.

June, light headed, bubbly and bigmouthed, treats her seventy year old father like a small child, nagging and scolding and regimenting, yet she is all he has left of the forty-eight years he was married to the most wonderful woman in the world who was taken by the Good Lord - who alone knows where or why - ten years previously. Alfred suffers his daughter's patting, pushing and prodding in near silence just as he suffers her constant reference to him in the plural as though he was a littler of kittens. What a contrast with his explosive forensic displays at the Pensioners Union! There Alfred is the stirring firebrand, the prophet, the doomsayer, the rabble rouser, the castigator of the unrighteous, the unfit and the unready.

Alfred's quiet toastmaking is interrupted by two sounds: one of June rousing and raising her sensorious self above his head, and the other of a man loudly hawking and spitting in the street outside. Alfred takes two steps to the kitchen window, draws back the yellowed plastic curtain and sees in the bright daylight of King George Street the Poet, his cut and battered hand on the gatepost for support, bowing low, his head almost between his knees. The white hand leans on the gatepost as the hawking continues to wrack his body, then, when it subsides, the shaggy head slowly raises revealing to the unseen audience the mottled purple face, roary red tearfilled eyes and long swinging string of spittle suspended from the cracked lower lip. The Poet straightens himself, rubs a hand over his face, gingerly releases the gate post and lurches forward down the hill towards the harbour where Neilie the Wharf Rat is dreaming of drowning in a vat of Woods Navy and the Red Cross nowhere in sight.

"Good morning," June patronisingly sings from the kitchen doorway, where she has appeared in a turquoise quilted housecoat, "and how are we today?"

"Oh, hello dear," Alfred sighs as he lets the plastic curtain spring back into place and turns to face her.

It is impossible for him to believe that this woman in front of him came out of the other one who is gone, even less credible that he had any part in her making because she is so unlike both he and the Wonderful One. His searching eyes do not betray their intent, nor does his disbelief register in any line of his ancient road map of a face. At home in Number 16 King George Street, Alfred Petrie's visage is always blank, his eyes unflickering, his voice gentle and steady, his movements slow and deliberate.

"And did we have a good night's sleep?" June asks in her talking-to-dogs-and-babies-voice as she pats her father on the shoulder.

"Not bad, dear," he replies, wondering if maybe a cuckoo had dropped this one in the next when he and the Wonderful One had not been looking.

"That's good," she says in a lullabye tone, "and we musn't forget to have our walk this morning, must we?"

Numb with condescension, Alfred simply nods his white head. June, who is up and about early today and does not have to be at Jacob's Better Priced Clothing Mart until nine o'clock, retreats, a clinical smile painted over her pink gash of a mouth, to her room where she listens to the gabble and babel of the "Good Morning Show" and she polishes her nails.

Four streets seaward, June Petrie's co-worker at Jack Jacob's store, Gloria Goodman, is being frantically and gratefully ravished by Paul Newman, or, to be more accurate, she is ravishing him. Since late last night, when she went to bed with the golden itch

17

following a quarrel with her boyfriend of the evening, Gloria Goodtime has been spending a long hot and restless night of one almost after another and now, having pursued the naked and glistening Mr. Newman for an eternity of near misses, she has finally wrestled him to the ground and is thrusting her sweating, yearning, aching self upon him. By anybody's standards Gloria is an attractive young woman, particularly for those whose preferences lean toward the buxom, the softly plump, the well upholstered. She is short, which tends to emphasise her slightly stocky appearance, with smooth, tight, pink buttocks, gorgeous golden legs, and very large perfectly globular white breasts. Her face is full and rosy cheeked, her mouth wide and sensuous - sometimes revealing her lovely white teeth in a marvelous impish smile - and her eyes when they are open are large and twinkling. She has shoulder length soft straw coloured hair which swishes about her ears and under her ever so slightly double chin where, the initiated know, is an endearing patch of soft down. Gloria's ample body is twisted and intertwined with the moist bedclothes as she desperately struggles with Mr. Newman, and her upper lip is beaded with perspiration, her breathing hot and rapid and her sweaty, pudgy hands are almost tearing the pillow around which she has thrown her hungry arms.

With her sheets askew and flimsy pink nightie half removed by her exertions, Gloria is truly a warming sight for anyone who understands this coaltown or the world in which it has been dumped; only ice-cold, stone-hewn, miserable, grudging, crimped curmudgeons could look upon this scene and not catch their breath or have their heart miss a beat. Sad to tell, therefore, all those who are quite properly cheering her on that the outrageously alien, unwelcome and raucus alarm clock has, with not an atom of sensitivity in its mechanical soul, pierced shrill and jarring through the warm haze of fantasy and awakened our dreamer at the precise moment of Mr. Newman's entrance through the gates of heaven.

The big yellow dog which hangs around the grounds of Saint Bridgit's rectory opens one eye, takes in the rapidly growing day, stretches, stands, scratches and howls loudly. It is the sign to the occupants that it is time for God's, as well as man's, work to be done. Inside the rambling old glebe house, one of the occupants is astir without the yellow dog's assistance. Daisy Gracie, the priest's housekeeper, has already donned heavy dressing gown and slippers, shuffled down stairs, turned up the furnace and put the kettle on the big black stove. Now she sits stonily and hatchet-faced, waiting for the kettle to boil so she can have her essential infusion of morning tea which she makes thick, dark and strong. Her charges are still abed; Father Ransome and Father Allen yet in dreamland - the former single-handedly building a huge new church, the latter reluctantly but irreligiously wallowing in impurity. But whitened, ancient Father MacIntyre wrenched from the soft wandering dream of the Holy Land is mistily gazing at the ceiling and praying fervently for redemption of mankind and of Father Allen in particular whom he knows from intimate conversations with that gentleman, is quite against his will, "troubled by his balls."

Father Ransome awakens first, as he hears the wail of the dog, sits bolt upright and leaps out of bed to a Godly, busy and very important day. Not only has the Lord instructed Father Ransome to administer to the sick, the poor, and the needy of his own faith but he has commanded him to also observe the Protestants (whose own pastors are, to his way of thinking, notoriously negligent in their spiritual and temporal duties) - and, further, to ensure that the administration of the town is conducted in accordance with the most honest, upright and efficient procedures. In his spare time, which the Lord knows is little enough considering the burdensome charges he has made of his son, Father Ransome has been requested by the Almighty to cast a critical and not infrequent eye over the government of the province and of the nation as a whole and, where he finds it wanting, to express himself in no uncertain terms to any who will - or have no choice but to - listen.

In the next room, Father Allen is grateful for the canine's wailing since it swiftly removes him from his unclean dreams and into the land of the living. So strong is the sunlight on his face as he awakens that, for a second, the young priest imagines he is back in the jungles of Nicaragua where the Bible was not his only weapon and God's works could not always be carried out with soft words and sweet reason. He dresses, begs forgiveness to Almighty God for his recurring transgressions, and goes down to a breakfast, not of fruit and pemmican, but of Daisy Gracie's stodgy and lumpish porridge.

Not to be outdone lest it should be spread abroad they are more tardy than their Romish breathern, the protestant clergy, too, are stirring and making ready for tending of the frequently woolly, often bleating, but not always obedient flock. The Reverend Horace Cameron Day, whose facial resemblance to Ian Paisley is remarkable, is, one assumes, unlike Dr. Paisley, shaving his jutting chin with only thoughts of bringing mankind closer together. Rev. Day is the town's leading ecumenist. His mission in life is to spread love, tolerance and understanding wherever he goes, but his efforts are somewhat impaired by the manner in which he approaches his sacred task. He believes that if people will not love each other voluntarily then they must be forced to love one another. Cameron Day is overflowing with good motives and underflowing with tact and diplomacy. He has recently lost half of his church elders who resigned because when they suggested to him, during a meeting of the boys club, that the meeting should be adjourned due to the untimely passing of one of their number, he growled at them: "Let the dead bury the dead. We have work to do." His recently having called the pregnant daughter of one of the elders up to the altar during the Sunday service to use her as a living example of forgiveness was appreciated even less and his devotion of at least half of the parish Bulletin to pungent comments on Chile, the penitentiary system and nuclear power have all contributed to his congregation having recorded a negative growth rate of such proportions that the dark, respectable and wood panelled presbytry is having sacramental kittens.

Captain William Mercer, this bright and beckoning morning, uncomplicated and singled-minded as ever, is, in his smart and brushed uniform, surveying the back yard - and regaling the sparkling ocean beyond with a version of "Bringing in the Sheaves" which is only slightly flat and, as a consequence, a little too joyful and not sufficiently heart-rending for a service at the Citadel.

A matter of a few doors away, the Reverend Clarence Hines is, between mouthfuls of bacon, doing what he has done in his dreams all night: trying out high sounding, poetic, prophetic and profound phrases with which to generously lard sermons, speeches, eulogies and general conversation. "Death is to the dead what life is to the living," he intones at his wife as she pours his tea. She smiles tolerantly; after twenty-four years there is nothing she can do to change things now. "And life," continues her husband to her retreating back, "is not unlike a cup of tea which we drink to the dregs, there to finally see what we have truly left behind us."

On 12 South wall, three miles out under the ocean and deep in the black bowels of the Jubilation colliery, Popeye MacDougall, Willie Ross and Danny "treacle" Fraser are taking a spell. A little above and ahead of them Joe "Priest" MacLennan is operating the great Anderton Shearer which is slowly, inexorably eating its way into and along the coal face. Behind them stands Buck MacPhee Junior, the overman, cautiously regarding the roof, while a little further along the incline are "Pope" Leo MacLeod and Steamie Kelly. Treacle gestures over his shoulder with a grin and Willie and Popeye twist their heads so they can listen in. Every day Pope and Steamie are arguing and sparring, the former representing the powers of goodness and light, the latter those of chaos, disorder and irreverance.

"Ah, Christ all frigging Mighty," growls Steamie, "Jesus, did I ever tie on a Christly drunk last night. Me jeesly head is ready to blow open."

"My heaven, Steamie," Pope says indignantly, his eyes averted upwards, "whatever would the good Lord think if he would hear the way you're talking now?"

"Listen Pope," Steamie replies savagely, "there's t'ings goin on down in this here pit he don't know fuck all about!"

The men up the wall laugh out loud and Steamie sends a gob of spit flying in their direction. They retreat and regroup a few yards further on.

The doctors are also awake now. Dr. Donald Donelly has been up all night, on call at St. Michael's Hospital and, between a delivery, one heart attack, two cases of minor cuts and bruises (from the same fight), twelve cups of rank, black coffee and a few scarcely comprehended chapters of the only non-medical book to be found, he has been thinking with increasing longing of the wet green fields of Dunquin, the endless golden beach at Inch, the busy little harbour at Dingle, the mists around the top of Mount Brandon and the publican's smiling, bright red haired daughter in Annascual. Two of his colleagues, Dr. Singh and Dr. Hoque are breakfasting silently, solemnly over honey and toast and tea spiced with cardamon, cloves and cinnamon. At this time in the morning they are barely possessed of the faculty of speech, but after an hour's warming up they will frantically, excitedly, be harranguing the world at large on every subject under the sun and driving the entire hospital staff to distraction. To their less charitable colleagues they are known respectively as "The Mouth" and "The Machine Gun," but for all the complaints about their volubility and garralous pestering, they are the first to be invited to a party, the first to be called in emergency, the first to be approached for favours. These two oriental gentlemen have in the few years they have spent in the coaltown, been taken to the hearts of the people. Their older colleague Dr. S. Winstanley (nobody knows his first name) commands no such respect or affection. Cold, aloof, aging contentedly alone, he rises today, as every day, coolly gleeful that with the number of beds he has cornered for his patients he has earned five hundred dollars even before he cracks open his egg.

As Dr. Winstanley slowly drives his gleaming grey Cadillac towards the hospital he notices a shambling figure, turning off Main Street and into the dark little alley which leads to the wharf. He, of course, takes no further notice, but he has just witnessed the disappearing back of our literary friend the Poet, who is now only minutes away from refuge and sustenance.

Neilie the Wharf Rat has been awake for an hour since the first pinpoints of gold crept through the cracks under the doors of Gillis' warehouse and stabbed into his misty and now almost unseeing eyes. He puts on his bent glasses, their lenses cracked, dirty and as thick as the bottoms of beer bottles and lies there massaging his arms and legs until the circulation comes creeping slowly back. Then, when he is able to get up and move, he shuffles to his secret corner and lights the Coleman stove - his most treasured possession - and puts the water on to boil for tea. The kettle is one he was given long ago, by a kind-hearted housewife, the teapot, an old battered can of whose previous contents there now remains no indication, and the brew itself is concocted from water from the tap in the back wall of the fish plant, three used tea bags rescued from the garbage can behind the Melody Restaurant and a small bottle of vanilla extract which mysteriously jumped into his hand yesterday in a commercial emporium.

Just then the Poet enters. He settles down by the stove to share the life-giving brew. Their conversation is for the most part parallel and simultaneous; Neilie's monosyllabic and barely intelligible, Lemuel's drawling and theatrical.

"Wake," states Lem with a gesture to the window high in the wall, "for morning in the bowl of night, has fired the rock that puts the stars to flight and see the hunter of the east has caught the Sultan's turret in a noose of light."

Father Allen, his face tanned and handsome, is sitting back in his chair - its two front legs in the air - with his big black boots up on the table, and is absently staring out of the window into the sunny morning. Bronzed and stocky, Father Allen is powerful and slightly threatening like a coiled spring or a lurking predator. Although he is only twenty-nine his hair is iron grey around the ears and his face is deeply lined. His wide mouth is grimly set - at first giving the appearance of a permanent smile but the hard grey eyes warn against such an assumtpion. Here is a man who is volatile and unpredictable and is generally considered by his fellow clergy to be a bit risky; Father Ransome describes him as unsafe

The shiningly pious and freshly scrubbed Father Ransome is earnestly pouring over the morning newspaper, frowning every now and then and censoriously shaking his head and clucking his tongue over the many foibles of a world of sinners. He notes the fall of the dollar; he observes the Dow Jones industrial average; he marks the impending tax increase; he absorbs and files the riots, the demonstrations, the failure of the Summit, the winning of the Miss Nude World contest and the notice of the special meeting of Town Council to which, he has grimly determined, he will make strenuous and compelling representations.

The world, alas, daily growing more wicked and inept, may do as it pleases but its doings will not go undetected, not escape the ever vigilant eye of Father Ransome who alone - in company with the Holy Father (and Father Ransome sometimes wonders about *him*) - knows what needs to be done to set the universe aright. This walking repository of virtue, this man of God whose confidence is abundant and who does not in the least fear to judge lest he be judged, presents a striking contrast indeed with his younger, unsafe colleague. Father Ransome is taller than the rebellious Father Allen but is thinner; where the former is tanned, he is ruddy; where Allen is lithy, he is gaunt; where one is arrogant, the other is imperious. Father Ransome's sparse but still jet black hair is carefully plastered down and over his pink scalp and shines with old fashioned smelly brilliantine. His hands are large, white and elegant with long fingers and manicured nails and his X ring is of gold and obviously made to order. His clerical garb, while black as the blackest night, has a flair not seen in the dress of his colleagues; an ecclesiastical pizazz subtly created by the fact that it is all made-to-measure from the best cloth and hangs on him as on a gentleman of fashion. There should be nothing shabby about the Lord's work or his servants as far as Father Ransome is concerned!

Father MacIntyre sits quietly swaying in the old rocking chair, happily smoking an Export A and gazing blankly at the bare wall in front of him. His little bit of hair is fluffy and snow white, his old face pale and sagging, his lips fleshy, wet and blue, his teeth yellow and rotting. Cigarette ash has tumbled down his collar and into his lap and his feeble attempts to brush it away have ground it into the coarse black cloth. A few dribbles of porridge adorn his shirt front where they overlie yesterday's egg and gravy stains. His fly is undone. One pudgy, wrinkled hand lies over his little pot belly while his right hand is raised to his face, the cigarette between the first two fingers, and the thumb absently scraping a large patch of white underchin bristle which was missed by the morning's razor.

Gloria Goodman toddles into Jacob's Better Priced Clothing Mart like a bitch in heat. All male heads turn as she clicks up the street and turns in the doorway. From the windows of Cordopoulus Shoe Repair across the road the eyes of Spiro and his assistant Lonnie Walker watch hungrily, and just up by the Oasis Restaurant, Jackie MacKinnon studies the action in the mirror of his taxi. There is an overwhelming sensation of sensuality in Main Street this randy morning and every little thing about Gloria Goodtime Goodman proclaims to the rooftops, where even the pigeons are getting frisky, exactly what is on her mind. She is made up and turned out even more voluptuously than usual with turquoise eyeshadow, passion pink lipstick, long black and fluttering false eyelashes, and a carefully placed beauty spot.

If Gloria's low-cut sweater and skirt were any tighter she would be unable to breathe; they are both of a thin, soft, pale pink wool which reveals almost as much as is possible without violating the criminal code. So blessed is Gloria in the thoracic regions that a bra is an absolute necessity, but it is so sheer and skimpy that it barely disturbs the smooth surface of the sweater except where her pronounced nipples impertinently, brazenly, announce themselves to a gaping and often breathless world. Her perfectly moulded and rythmically slung buttocks need no such support and it is abundantly clear to those who know about such things that she wears no panties, for there is not a line, crease nor ripple visable through the snugly fitting skirt. Jackie MacKinnon sighs and wishes he was young. Spiro Cordopoulus' heart aches and Lonnie Walker's innards groan with longing.

From Gloria's delicate white lobes swing long, glittering earrings which not only flash as they twirl but tinkle too, like little love bells, and, if not in perfect time at least in no discordant manner, the fire engine red stiletto heeled shoes clik-clak in a merry, horny dance setting off her lovely calves to perfection. Slightly cheap and somewhat gaudy may be her taste, a touch less than demure her deportment, but as she bounces into her drab place of employment, carrying the goods and the golden itch with her, she defies any man in whose veins good red blood still flows not to feel, upon drinking in this vision of femininity, some slight stirrings of life.

The sun is climbing high now in the wispy sky. the smoke is climbing from a thousand chimneys, the trains, cars, busses and people are moving about and around the little town. Main Street is in business again.

Shaker MacEachern awakens very late, his dreams have been very disturbing indeed and have caused him much discomfort. Although his dreams were successively of capturing and possessing Sheila MacLeod, Wendy Hillier, Margaret MacDonald, Charlene Young, Freda MacNeil, Marie Sullivan and even Hilda Poirier, they were all as desperately bone dry as a rock in the midsummer sun. Shaker, his blood raging, polevaults out of bed and rushes down the hall to see if Evelyn the lodger is in her room. While Shaker subscribes in his urgency to the notion of any port in a storm, he finds the door locked and the port closed to traffic until further notice. Breathing heavily, he phones Edna Sharpe his often reliable, but somewhat venerable widow who lives on the next street. Criminally insensitive to his great need she informs him she is just off to town and adds in a comforting tone that Shaker should take a cold shower. He slams down the phone, cursing, blaspheming, swearing on every oath that his will shall not be thwarted.

The sound of the splashing water in the MacEachern's shower is truly the final sign to the coaltown that absolutely everybody is awake and that the day has commenced its proceedings.

Russell Buker / Judique

Russel Buker was born in 1939 in the U.S., pitched semi-pro baseball while in high school and attended the University of New Hampshire. He farmed in Kennebunkport, Maine, before moving for good to Cape Breton in 1972 where he works at being a self-sufficient farmer. His poetry has appeared in **The Antigonish Review** and he has studied Creative Writing at the Banff School of Fine Arts in Alberta.

Eminent domain was the reason for leaving Maine and after much searching we saw our place and bought it. An island seeker doesn't have to be told he has arrived at the right place.

TWO LETTERS

Hello
I know it's late
You
should see me
bald
rapidly losing teeth
sitting
on a new bale of hay
cutting
a hang toenail
Fly
buzzing around a bare
light-
bulb it is
fall
again for you and I
amble
around looking for things
to stomach
while my grandfather
lies
licking air And an
uncle
sits staring his
eyes
remind me of two
stars
in my life that
I
accumulated
hope
I have come too far
to be
afraid of gift giving
especially
my children while

I still
feel the tug down
my light-
shaft for more earth

Russell Buker

SAILOR LEAVE

The pasture's all moss but cran
berries and popple
and an ache will be near
where the house was
I climb   climb with my little girl
away from the sea
Where can I go   Cape
Breton   where can I go
Home again with black
spruce and farm golden juniper
calling from the road
Oh   convince me I'm a sailor
Where can I go
It's quiet here   I'm
forty below
sea's above   spruce hen's
wind is gone
to lay in some light fog
and I climb   climb to the night
with boots that are wet   hands
that are more   Cape
Breton   where can I go

Russell Buker

WHITE SAIL

Oh yes there are boats
all around my house
a large grain of salt
my daughters' scissoring
Old lady think of me
as fisherman Knit
me a sweater for the famous
sea Lengthen the cuff
Cover this curl from
perpetual motion in an
astative ocean Here
knicks in my hand from hooks
and bait I get knocked
flat from swelling I didn't
see How else do I know
I'm coming home Sugar
sure measure me I don't
fish your island but we
work the same Novy
hulls and I feel
your osseous hands
wringing pleasure to me
and I, favored, know need
of your capacity — then
I would believe my fable
leave your work
to you and the wool wave

Russell Buker

Silver Donald Cameron / D'Escousse

Silver Donald Cameron was born in Toronto in 1937 and lived in Vancouver, Fredericton, California, London and Buckinghamshire before settling down for good in D'Escousse, on Isle Madame along the south shore of Cape Breton. He received an M.A. from the University of California and a Ph.D. from the University of London. From 1978 to 1980, Cameron was writer-in-residence at the University College of Cape Breton.

He founded a short-lived alternate newspaper called **The Mysterious East** and later edited two important literary supplements **(Voices Down East)** for Halifax's **Fourth Estate.** Cameron's non-fiction books include: **Faces of Leacock** (1967), **Conversations with Canadian Novelists** (1973), **The Education of Everett Richardson** (1977) and **Seasons in the Rain** (1978).

In 1980 Cameron published **Dragon Lady,** his first novel, an intriguing blend of social criticism and adventure. An upcoming novel, **Adam Bolliver** concerns a young man who sets out to sail a barrel from Lunenburg to Bermuda. "Snapshot" originally appeared in **The Atlantic.**

Silver Donald Cameron is married to Lulu and along with "a small arrogant son who comes by it honestly" they live in a giant old renovated house in D'Escousse.

> *What is Cape Breton anyway? A good place to shed the plastic nonsense and random noise which bedevil us and to contemplate ultimate matters: struggle, loss, beauty, love, pain. Cape Breton is a good place to wrestle with failure, emptiness, and death. After one has come to terms with these massive darknesses, perhaps one is at last ready to value the light, to live with joy and grace and appetite, to make pictures, to make books, to make music, to make love.*

Snapshot: The Third Drunk

by Silver Donald Cameron

The man on the left is Phonse. The man on the right is Wilf. The man in the center appears to be drunk.

Falling down drunk. Head lolling, hair lank. Slumping between Phonse and Wilf. His knees loosely bent. Held up by an arm over Phonse's shoulders, another over Wilf's, each of them grasping his hand to keep him from falling. The drunk wears a dark suit. Phonse and Wilf in shirt-sleeves are grinning, grinning too heartily. Even in this dog-eared, wrinkled old photograph, the well-dressed drunk looks pale.

* * *

Phonse stamps on the plank floor of the Anchor Tavern, roaring for another.

"See 'im," grunts Jud. "Says it's dear, but he's havin' another."

"Didn't make beer money today anyways," Phonse says. "Got just about enough for a chowder, that's all."

"Them scales is wrong," Jud repeats. "We had that old box full up last week and they said it was two thousand pounds. Now we get half-filled and they say fifteen hunnert."

And the smell: the pungent, malty tavern, the sour reek of the fish-meal plant, sweat and tobacco, and beneath all, like a bass figure in an old song, the salt nip of the beaches and kelp, and cold spray over the stones . . .

"What the Jesus you gonna do?" Phonse shrugged. "Not like the old days. Didn't need no money in the old days." He winks at me. "You should of been here then, boy. By the Jesus, we had some right roarin' times in them days."

"Need money now," Jud said.

"You can't starve a fisherman, though," Phonse insisted. "Old Wilf Rattray used to say that all the time, ye can't starve a fisherman. D'you mind old Wilf, Jud?"

"Can't really say so. I was just a kid."

"He must have drowned in - let's think now. In the big storm in sixty-three, just before Christmas. He was on a wooden side dragger out o' North Sydney."

"I was about ten then."

"Must of been that sixty-three storm. Wilf was at Reg Munroe's wake in sixty-two, and there wasn't anyone from here drowned off a dragger for a couple of years after sixty-three, I don't believe."

"I got a sort of vague recollection of him."

"Oh Jesus, he was a great old boy. Your old dad there, he'd mind him, don't you, Alfred?"

"Great old boy?" Alfred rumbled. "He was a god-damn Jonah, was Rattray. Black Foot Rattray, we used to call him."

Phonse winked at me again. "Call 'em Black Foot when they're so goddamn unlucky their feet get dirty in the bath."

"Black Foot Rattray," muttered Alfred, shaking his head.

"Great old fellow all the same," Phonse insisted. "He wa'n't so much unlucky as stupid. Sign him on as engineer, he'd go down and tinker with the engine. A tinkerer, that's what he was. No matter how sweet she'd been runnin', Rattray'd have her bustin' head gaskets and burnin' out bearings the first day at sea."

"I shipped along of him once," Alfred declared. "Never again. That was the trip he cut off his finger in the winch, an' Jesus, he'd *already* had us back home once with engine trouble."

Phonse started to laugh. "He was a Jonah, right enough. But he was a barrel of fun at a party. We had good parties in them days."

Alfred chuckled. "We did so," he murmured. "We had some parties, all right."

* * *

No bullshit: there is no bullshit in Widow's Harbor. Drifting along the coast with a little money and no plans, all my futures behind me, I followed the back roads off the back roads and discovered Widow's Harbor at the dead end of a rocky peninsula thrusting into the Atlantic like an arthritic finger. In Toronto, someone was editing manuscripts. Someone else was meeting the Senator for lunch at the Westbury. Someone else was agreeing to be at the television studio a little before 3:00 for makeup. Someone else.

As for me, I was sitting on a precarious lobster trap at the end of a sagging wharf, sharing a bottle of Abbey Rich Canadian Port ($1.40) with Phonse and Alfred Nickerson. After that there was a dozen of Tenpenny and some talk about gill-netting and long-lining and the lobster season, and then there was some McGuinness rum, and then there must have been something resembling a decision not to drive on that night. Around noon the next day I found myself surrounded by clean flannelette sheets with the threads showing, in a small, white, slant-ceilinged room, and when I stumbled downstairs I discovered Phonse's wife Laura making lunch for the kids who would be coming home from school. Laura snickered at my headache and poured some black coffee. Phonse had gone fishing at 4:00 a.m.

"He's usually away by three," she said, "but I guess you fellows really tied one on last night. Phonse, he was some full."

There seemed no reason to leave the next day, or the next, and when I found the shack across the road was for rent, I took it. I could make enough to get by on if I were to run into Halifax every week or so with some radio talks, and I had friends in Widow's Harbor. It was a good place to read, talk, drink, and grow strong. In the scrubby woods, mushrooms erupted from the pine needles underfoot. I combed the beaches for driftwood to be converted to lamps for the shack. There were deer and rabbits to be hunted with Purvis, my landlord; nets to be mended with Phonse and Alfred; and radio talks to be written about these things and others. I found I was living comfortably on about a sixth of my Toronto salary, and at that I was making a good thousand dollars a year more than Phonse or any of the others.

Widow's Harbor can afford no bullshit: it lives too near the bedrock of health and illness, shelter and food, death and tax sales. No one can hide: the snow-filled easterlies and the neighbors' tongues scour every cranny. Toronto's bruises soon fade. They are not, after all, catastrophes: on this bare rock, along this open coast, where even death is contemptibly familiar, the loss of a salary or a lover stands revealed as a petty misfortune at most.

*   *   *

"Come on over for some breakfast," says Phonse, shaking my shoulder, "and get a wiggle on. Supposed to be a blow coming up tonight, but we'll make a few sets before she hits."

Two shirts, heavy sweater, pea jacket; long johns, two pairs of pants; extra socks, rubber boots. Crossing the road in the coal-black night, slithering on ice, still stupid with sleepiness. Phonse frying bacon and eggs. The kitchen clock: 2:15.

"You usually have bacon and eggs?"

"Me? Naw, just bread and molasses and away I go. Don't usually have company for breakfast, though."

"For Christ's sake, Phonse."

"Stop bitchin' and eat."

Down the snowy road to Alfred's, plastic bags of bread and molasses in our hands. Grunts of greeting, and down to the wharf. Fluffy snow on the *Harvey and Sisters,* a sweet, forty-foot Cape Islander with a high flaring bow; she set Alfred back four grand. Lines cast off, the Buick V-8 sends a throaty purr through the big hot stack spearing up through the wheelhouse. Frost on the windshield. A light chill wind ruffles the harbor.

The purr turns to a heavy burble as we clear the harbor mouth line up the yellow leading lights, and make an hour's straight steaming to the fishing grounds on Widow's Bank. Desultory talk. Phonse pisses over the side, back in the wide cockpit among the waiting tubs of trawl.

Then overboard go the highflyers, buoys with tall flagstaffs, easy to see even in the eerie pre-dawn, and the trawl pays out, the baited hooks every fathom or so, and a highflyer at the end. Steaming back up the long lines for an hour and a half at sunrise, and hauling in fish.

"Another taxi driver, Jud."

"Why do you call pollack taxi drivers?"

"Dunno. We just do, that's all. Oho! Them big steakers is what

35

we like to see."

Monkeyfish and dogfish to be thrown back. Cod and flounder. A day of heavy hauling, icy water everywhere, with one coffee break, bobbing around in the fo'c'sle with the engine shut off. As the short day closes in, Alfred spins the wheel, heads *Harvey and Sisters* toward shore.

And Phonse with a deft slash rips each fish from vent to gill and throws it to Jud, who scoops the guts out and overboard in one swift motion, tossing the fish into the bin in the center of the cockpit. They gut a fish every six seconds. Every forty feet, regular as dripping blood, the guts hit the ocean, and the gulls come, a few at first, then a crowd, finally a swarm, dropping like dive bombers on the livers and intestines and half-digested mackerel. Ten minutes ago there wasn't a gull in sight; now hundreds hover over *Harvey and Sisters*.

The wind is rising, the white caps multiply, the promised blow is coming. Numb with cold already, I hunch in the wheelhouse, watching the first flakes of snow fly over the black water. Alfred has swung a hinged bench into place, and sits high behind the windshield, holding her steady by the compass now, back to Widow's Harbor. Phonse and Jud stamp in, shaking like wet dogs.

"Son of a bitch," Jud observes.

"Yessir," Phonse agrees. "Yessir, she's all of that."

Just outside the harbor, the storm hits: the sea begins boiling, the shriek of the wind sails in above the throb of the V-8. A whitecap foams into the cockpit.

"Self-bailing," Phonse reassures me. Another whitecap froths over the stern.

"Runnin' her a little close, Alfred," says Alfred.

"Save us some scrubbin'," Jud philosophizes. And we are in, inside the harbor, with the wind down to nothing and the sea no more than a chop. The motor dies down, and *Harvey and Sisters* idles over to the fish buyers' dock. After Jud and Phonse fork the fish into the crates for weighing, we will scour the boat clean and bait the trawl for the next day, coiling it carefully in the tubs so it will pay out smoothly.

"What's the time gettin' to be, there?" Phonse asks me.

"Two-fifteen."

"Good enough," Jud nods. "Be home by seven-thirty, quarter to eight."

"Might even be time for a beer," Phonse reflects for a moment. "Do you think, Alfred?"

"Might be," says Alfred.

* * *

You can't starve a fisherman. In the old days you didn't need money.

"Why, sure," says Phonse, draining a beer glass. "Look now, everyone had his own cow, so there was your milk and butter and cheese. Everybody had a few chickens, so there was your eggs and some of your meat. Everybody had a kitchen garden, so there was your vegetables, and the women got enough in preserves—well, you seen Laura's preserves even now, ain't you? We got enough there for two years even if we never *ever* got anything out of the garden this year. And there was always deer in the woods, more 'n now, and rabbits and ducks, sometimes a moose. You didn't have to be any too fussy about the season then, either. Then you had your wild berries—blueberries and cranberries and blackberries and bakeapples—you ever see bakeapples growin' wild? They look like a little orange hat on a green spike, just one to a bush, the swamps was full of 'em. Some folks had pigs and sheep, and the sea was always full of fish and lobsters, and we wa'n't too upset about the season on them, neither."

"You still aren't," I said, remembering an evening with a dozen of the biggest, reddest, juiciest out-of-season lobsters I ever saw.

"So they say," Phonse countered, with a huge grin. "Course I wouldn't know. You take a chance now, you can lose your boat and your car and pay a big fine. I wouldn't fool around with that sort of stuff."

"Christ, no," I said, shaking my head. "Wouldn't be worth it."

Alfred burst out laughing.

In the old days, the cows were put out to summer pasture on Meadow Island, in the harbor mouth. You took a rowboat and two men: one rowed, and the other held the cow's head up, and the cow swam over to the island. Horses will swim without coaxing, but you have to help a cow.

"I mind one time," said Phonse, "I had to go get the cow at the end of the summer. Well, Jesus! Spent two days on that goddamn island and do you think I could catch that old son of a whore? No sir, couldn't get *near* it. 'Course I always hated that Christly cow. I'm not a goddamn farmer, I'm a fisherman. But my old mom, she hadda have a cow, so of course I hadda get it out to the island in the spring and back in the fall. But I couldn't even catch the bastard.

"So I come back with six other fellows and a motor boat, and we cornered the bugger and put a rope around her neck and led her down to the beach, but when we got her there do you think she'd go in the water? Not on your Jesus life she wouldn't. We all got in the boat and sagged on the rope, and she wouldn't budge an inch. Just dug her old hooves down in the sand and that was that.

"Well, I got mad. I said to myself, I don't care if I kill that cow or break its neck or whatever the hell happens I don't care. So I cracked the old throttle full out, and I let out all the slack and went roarin' out into the harbor, and that rope come taut and 'bout jerked that cow's head right off. She drove her hooves down in the sand to the knees and then she buckled, just come a-flyin' up in the air like a cork out of a bottle and hit the water about thirty feet out. I never let up on the throttle one bit till I got to the other side, I like to *drowned* that cow, and she was comin' up and down and sideways and wallowin' around, her eyes buggin' out, you never saw anything like it. Jesus, I said to myself that's the last time I ever have anything to do with that cow; and it was. Vet killed her before the next spring come around."

I was laughing too hard to speak.

"It's true, honest to God. And we had some parties, too."

"We did," sighed Alfred. "Oh, I guess we did."

"Remember that time Muriel Naugler and Loretta O'Leary got loaded at the beach party?"

"Lord, Lord," said Alfred.

"Jesus, that was some funny. The two of them got lit, and Loretta, she'd been foolin' around with Harry Naugler, and Muriel started to come onto her about it. So Loretta gave *her* a scandalizin', said if she was any kind of a wife to him there wouldn't be nothin' anyone could do about it, and Muriel—well, I guess she got right savage wild then. So she starts screamin' about how she's got a dose of clap from Harry bringin' it home from Loretta, and Loretta says it was Harry give it to her in the first place, so who'd he get it from, that's what she wants to know, and before anybody can say Boo they're clawin' at each other and tearin' off each other's clothes and pullin' hair and I don't know what all, and they're practically bareass to the weather—and all the guys standin' around, you know, and cheerin' and watchin' and havin' a great old time."

"What a night," sighed Alfred.

"T'was the women broke it up, but it must of taken them a good half hour. Those days," Phonse explained, "used to have parties someplace or other every night, practically. Nothin' else *to* do. There wa'n't no television, and you couldn't get nothin' on the radio, and the movies was a travelin' affair, used to come here once every two weeks, so what else could ye do?"

"The wakes was the best," Alfred opined. "D'ye mind Reg Munroe's wake?"

"Guess I do, " declared Phonse. "T'was me picked up the coffin."

* * *

The cable from Halifax was very specific: TRAWLER ATLANTIC STAR RAMMED AND SUNK BY FREIGHTER HALIFAX HARBOR, it said, REGINALD MUNROE KILLED STOP REMAINS SHIPPED CNR MONKSTOWN CHARGES COLLECT STOP PLEASE ARRANGE COLLECTION REMAINS YOUR END STOP SINCEREST REGRETS DEEPEST CONDOLENCES THIS TRAGEDY STOP CORONER CITY OF HALIFAX.

Phonse had been living with Reg's sister Alice, and while Alice comforted her mother, Phonse offered to take his pickup truck the fifty miles to Monkstown and bring Reg's corpse home.

"Lord Jesus, I'll never forget it," said Phonse. "I got down there about noon, and didn't they have him standing on his head in the freight shed? They had boxes of stuff and bales and rolls of linoleum and bicycles, and tucked away right in the middle of it was old Reg, standin' on his head. I said to the agent he might at least let the fellow lie down, but he said he was stuck for space, it was just before Christmas, you know, and the shed was right jammed. It looked some strange, though, that coffin standin' on its head in all that pile of stuff." Phonse waved his glass in the air. "I b'lieve I'll have another."

"Me too," said Jud. "Phonse, I been wondering if there ain't some way we can get them scales checked."

"Dunno," said Phonse. "We could try, I guess."

* * *

I tried to imagine that trip home over the twisting road to Widow's Harbor with the corpse of your woman's brother behind you in the truck. Tried to imagine how you would secure it against the swings and bounces of that unkempt gravel road. What would the coffin look like? Plain, no doubt; would there be places to tie ropes?

The road winds through fifteen miles of forest with hardly a house to be seen, nothing but scrubby evergreens in low, folding country. Perhaps it would have been snowing, isolating Phonse and the corpse in a moving dome filled with drifting white flakes, settling a coating of fluff on the coffin so that in the truck's lights it would seem, as you looked over your shoulder through the rearview mirror, as though the coffin were becoming vague in outline, but alarmingly larger. The truck would be slipping and slithering around rock outcroppings, over little wooden bridges, past the entrances to abandoned logging roads. The coffin growing and fading.

Reg Munroe, fisherman. Alice's brother. Dead, as you could be dead yourself any day of your working life. Drowned. Lying back there in the back of the truck, cold and bloodless, chewed up by the big blade of some freighter.

The road comes down to the shore at Owl's Cove, a handful of houses clustered around a gas pump. The winter night comes down, and nothing shows but a scattered light; and after that, darkness, and surf beside the shore road, flying cloud and wind.

Phonse would have remembered, surely, all the ghost stories; the Spanish galleon in flames that enters one little cove every seventh year, the woman in white seen in the bows of a sinking windship just before the shipwreck, the tales of jealousy, torment, and murder recalled in minor-key folk songs as common as rocks along this shore. Once, fishing in a dragger on the Grand Banks, Phonse had found a human skull and a thigh bone in the nets: some poor sailor or fisherman drowned God knows how many decades or even centuries before, one of those lost at sea whose bodies were never found, nibbled clean by the codfish and sand fleas. The crew had gathered around on the afterdeck, passing the skull from hand to hand, uncertain what to do with it, and finally they had cast it back into the heaving sea whence it had come, to continue its long rest without further disturbance.

Reg Munroe, Alice's brother, fisherman, in a coffin in the back of the truck, a coffin growing larger as the snow continued to fall and the truck ground along the foaming edge of a cold sea . . .

* * *

"Jesus, Phonse!" I said. "That must have been some spooky ride."

"What's that?"

"Down from Monkstown with that coffin."

"Nah, shit, there wa'n't nothin' spooky about that. There was three of us went, and we took a bottle o' rum and got right polluted. Nah, somebody had to do it, an' I had the truck, that's all." He pulled at his beer and then wiped his lips on his checked shirt-sleeve. "But I tell you somethin' that wa'n't too canny when we got here."

A mile before Widow's Harbor they nearly went off the road, swerving to avoid a snow-shrouded figure trudging along. Stopping the truck to give the fellow a proper old scandalizing, Phonse was greeted by a cheery, "Evenin', Phonse, thanks a lot," and Jack Kavanaugh climbed into the crowded cab. "What's that in the back?"

"That's Reg Munroe's corpse."

"No," said Jack, "it ain't."

"It *is*," Phonse protested. "I picked him up in Monkstown. I got signed papers and everythin'."

"You look inside?"

"Hell, no."

"Well, it ain't Reg."

"How come you're so Jesus sure?"

"Well," said Jack, "Reg's body come in by sea this afternoon. I seen it. I'm just goin' in to the wake."

"Go away."

"It's *true*, Phonse."

"Snappin' Jesus Christ," said Phonse reverently. "Then who the hell have I got in the back of the truck?"

"It ain't Reg; that I do know."

"Well, Jesus," said Phonse grimly. "Soon's we get to town I think we better have a look at your, stranger."

Under a streetlight they stopped and opened the coffin. A man's face stared out at the sky. Snowflakes fell on his eyes: they did not melt. Phonse whistled low.

"My God, it's Teddy Lundrigan."

"I didn't even know Teddy was dead," Jack marveled.

"Nor I," Phonse agreed. "But I'd say he is, all right."

* * *

"That was some wake," Phonse chuckled. "By the Jesus, I was half cut already. I went right wild that night."

"I'll never forget you runnin' down them stairs with your trousers around your ankles," said Alfred.

"Oh my God, yes. Jesus, Ma Munroe was some savage when she come up and found all four couples ridin' together in them two beds. Didn't she take the broom to us, though?"

"Didn't she?"

"And Alice, she was right owly when she found out about me being up there with Stella."

"But she wa'n't nobody to talk. She was married to Buzz when you were livin' with her, wa'n't she, and him off workin' the lake boats in Upper Canada?"

"He always wanted to get me for a divorce," Phonse said. "But he never did." He turned to me. "But that ain't the best of it, or the worst, dependin' how you look at it."

"No?"

"Hell, no. See, later on that night we was just right out of our trees, you know? I don't think I was ever so full, never ever in my life. And old Wilf Rattray, him that drowned on that dragger, him and I heard that old Reg was cut up some when that freighter run them down. So what d'ye suppose we did?"

"What'd you do, Phonse?"

"We went into the room where the two corpses was, see, 'cause it was one big wake for the two of them, and we took old Reg out of his box and stripped him down. There was nothin' on his face, but his chest and legs was cut up pretty bad, all black and blue and the chest crushed in. Funny thing to see, all them cuts and him not bleedin'."

"Jesus, Phonse!"

"Well, hell, we didn't think old Reg'd mind. I wouldn't have minded, if it had of been me instead of him in that box. I mean, shit, we was old friends. Anyways, what d'ye suppose we did then?"

"Christ, Phonse, I hate to think."

"Why, we dressed him all up again, just like he was, and then old Wilf and me, we put one of his arms around each of our necks and had our pictures took."

"That's right," said Alfred, shaking his head. "That's right. God save us, you did that."

"Sure," said Phonse. "Sure we did. I still got the picture." He drew out his wallet.

* * *

The man on the left is Phonse. The man on the right is Wilf. The man in the center appears to be drunk.

Sheldon Currie / Reserve Mines

Sheldon Currie was born in Reserve Mines, attending high school there and in Glace Bay. After a short stint in the RCAF, he went to the College of Cape Breton and later St. Francis Xavier University, the University of New Brunswick and the University of Alabama. He has taught at Digby High School, St. Thomas University and is now with the English Department at St. Francis Xavier University where he is fiction editor of **The Antigonish Review.**

His first collection of short stores, **The Glace Bay Miner's Museum** appeared in 1981 and he has a forthcoming novel set in a Cape Breton mining community. "Lauchie and Liza and Rory" was originally published in **The Antigonish Review.**

Lauchie and Liza and Rory

by Sheldon Currie

I knew he'd take her in. I couldn't predict it, mind you, a minute before it happened, but when it did I said as a person often does: I knew it. Once it got to the point, he had to.

She wasn't even good looking. I can say that because she looked an awful lot like me. Red hair. Not the kind that glistens and goes good with green sweaters, but the other kind that looks like violin strings made of carrots. It had a part in the middle looked like an axe-cut, and it was pulled back hard and flat and tied at the back in a little ball you'd swear was nailed to the back of her neck. The same way I did it myself. She didn't exactly have buck teeth, but when her lips were closed her mouth was a little mound like she was keeping an orange peeling over her teeth. When she opened her mouth to talk you could see her teeth were round, and big, and almost the same color as her hair.

My brothers were identical twins, but as people they were day and night. Liza married Lauchie, the one everybody said was the good one. I could of told her, but I didn't. Even mother, a smart woman, thought Rory would be a gangster even after he went to work in the pit like everybody else. "He won't last," she said. "He'll get fired, if he don't get killed first, doing something foolish."

One Friday in the winter he left with a quart of rum and a dozen beer and a smile and never showed up 'til a week from Monday, out of a taxi, a cast on one leg from toe to hip, a smile on his face, two crutches, and two poles, and one ski.

"You fool," I said when I got him in the house and sat him down on the sofa. "You can't ski."

"Whyn't you tell me that 'fore I left?" he said, and, of course, the big smile.

"The beginning of the end," my mother said, with her eyebrows.

Lauchie went steady with Liza six months. Then he took her home to meet me and mother and Rory. Soon as she laid eyes on Rory she knew right then she made a mistake. How she knew I don't know. There wasn't a hair of difference between them. Rory knew it too. He shook hands with her. He never shook another person's hand in his life. He put out his big paw and she put her little red one in it, and he put his other hand on her shoulder; you could see her sink under it a fraction. You could almost see her eyes lock into his. "You'll like living here, Liza," he said. "It's a lot of fun if you look at it the right way."

"We'll not be living here," Lauchie said.

"Oh," said Rory. "I thought you were, next door, when the MacDonnell's move out."

"Well, we are," Lauchie said, "but *there* is not *here*. This is a duplex. Two different houses: one building."

"Some say it's a duplex," Rory said. "I say it's a company house."

"Well, what's the difference."

"Difference is simple," Rory said. "In a duplex you can't hear people drink water on the other side."

Lauchie wouldn't marry her 'til the MacDonnells moved out, so we had six months to watch her trying to make up her mind. Of course, she couldn't be sure Rory loved her. He might've been laughing at her. With him you couldn't tell for sure. I could, but I'd been watching him for years. Every time she came to the house he shook her hand, and he curled his middle finger so it stuck in her palm, but he did it so it looked like he was making fun of Lauchie, how formal he was when he introduced them. "Rory," he had said, "may I present to you my fiancee, Liza." And Rory shook her hand, like he did every time after, even after the marriage, and said, like an Englishman in the movies, "Awfully good of you to come," and everybody about doubled over laughing, except, of course, Lauchie, and, of course, our mother; she stood there and waited for things to get back to "normal".

So Liza and Lauchie got married; mother died - "mission accomplished, I suppose," Rory said. And they lived across the wall from us and honest to God we never heard a peep out of them 'til their kid was born. Then we heard the kid. They called him Rory. He cried for two years.

When he stopped, Liza started. Both our stairs went up the wall that separated us and I first heard her through that wall, sitting on her stairs, sobbing. After that I took to going over every day to console her, but she never admitted to anything, though she knew I knew. She caught on pretty quick how much alike we were. She talked about it one night we were playing cards, which we did every Friday. "If me and her," she said, meaning me, "If they got our x-rays mixed up, they wouldn't be able to tell which one had T.B." We all looked at her but Lauchie; he looked at his cards.

"What's it mean, anyway, T.B.?" he said.

"Tough biscuit," Rory said.

"You wouldn't need an x-ray to figure that out," I said, thinking to make a joke, but when I looked to Liza for her little smile, she was crying, and I knew there was no secret between us.

When little Rory was five and about to go to school they left him with us on the miner's vacation and went to Halifax to visit Liza's sister and get Lauchie's lungs looked at. "The little bugger needs a little fun before he goes to school," Rory said, and gave him every minute of his time, took him everywhere, showed him everything he could think of, even took him down the pit and showed him where him and his father worked.

When Lauchie and Liza came back, the boy wouldn't go back with them. They had to drag him back. Then he started school and every day he came home he came to the wrong gate and landed in our place. Lauchie would have to come over and drag him back.

"I thought I told you to come straight home."

"I forgot," he'd say.

He kept it up 'til we locked him out. We had to, to keep Lauchie from getting desperate. But he'd start again every time he went through a new phase of growing, until he got to be nine, and after that he wouldn't do his homework except at our place. He hated school, but he was first in his class because he did so much homework. Of course, Rory helped him; he couldn't resist; and when he got to grade nine and Rory couldn't help him anymore *he* started to teach big Rory. He taught him Algebra, French, Latin, Geometry, Chemistry, English, and God knows what all. He used to bring home the exams and Rory would do them and make high marks. "If I'd a known I was that smart I'd a stayed in school," he'd say. "Probably coulda been a teacher."

Of course he'd show off in the washhouse and turn it into a big joke. "What did you learn today, Rory?" somebody'd say.

"Today I learned that the sailor loves the girl," he'd say.

"And what have you got for homework?"

"For homework we have the girl loves the sailor, but I know it already, puellam nauta amat."

"What would that be in Gaelic?"

"In Gaelic, I couldn't say. I'm a Latin scholar. You'd have to ask me grandmother."

But he wouldn't carry it too far. He knew Lauchie felt bad and Rory wasn't a mean man, no matter how much he liked to make fun.

Once young Rory got to high school his home was nothing to him but bed and board. He had his tea first thing in the morning and last thing at night with us. He went into his side of the house for meals and bed. Nothing to do about it; he was too big then to make him. Lauchie had to put up with it. Liza sat on the stairs and sobbed. Rory felt bad but nothin he could do, and he couldn't help it that he enjoyed the boy so much. I just watched. I knew something had to happen.

When it happened, it happened very quietly. Of course, that was Liza's way; but I was surprised; I expected a big fight; after all , 17 years is a long time.

When young Rory graduated he got a big Knights of Columbus Scholarship and off he went to College. Liza picked the worst day she could find. It was coming down in buckets. She took her big suitcase and a kitchen chair and sat in the road between the two gates in her burberry and big-rimmed felt hat. It was the first time she ever looked beautiful. It was a Sunday. Both men were home. She went out after Mass and Rory and Lauchie, each in his own side of the house, opened the front doors and watched through their screen doors as she sat there in the mud. In those days there was no pavement, or even a ditch; the road came right up to the picket fence and she sat at the edge of it between the two gates. Talk about a sight. I can still see Rory standing there, peering through the screen, cup and saucer in his hand, sipping tea. And Lauchie on the other side, the same. I knew he would be. I just went over to check.

"What do you think, Lauchie?" I asked him.

"I think it has to be up to him."

And so it was. About six o'clock, Rory said to me. "You better go and tell her to come in. She'll stay there all night."

So in she came. Put on dry clothes and sat and had tea. She cried. They were tears of joy. She was ashamed of them, but couldn't help it. "I realize," she said, "that I'm probably not making anybody happy but myself. I can't help it."

After a few days when we all got the feeling it was settled for good, I moved over with Lauchie.

"Are you mad, Lauchie?" I asked him.

"Nobody to be mad at," he said. "I'd like to be mad. But, you know, it's not Rory's fault. He didn't encourage her; you know that. Just the opposite. Same for Liza. She tried for 17 years. It's not my fault. It's nobody's fault. Unless it's all our faults. It should of been fixed up 17 years ago when it started wrong. We all knew."

I certainly didn't know he knew.

"Well," I said, "young Rory will be surprised when he comes home for Christmas."

"I wonder," Lauchie said. "He's supposed to be smart too. I don't imagine college'll take it out of him that quick."

Don Domanski / Sydney

Don Domanski was born in 1950 and grew up in Sydney, Cape Breton. His ancestors had arrived there over three hundred years ago to work the coal mines and most of his family have been miners ever since. His heritage include Irish, Scottish, Welsh and Rumanian (his grandfather came from Transylvania).

Early influences on his work included Dylan Thomas, Robert Frost and Gerard Manley Hopkins, followed in recent years by Oriental and Surrealist poetry, East European and South American writings. His books include: **War in an Empty House** (1982), **Heaven** (1978), and **Cape Breton Book of the Dead** (1975). Domanski's poems have also been anthologized in **The Oxford Book of Canadian Verse, The Poets of Canada, Tributaries,** and **Storm Warning 2.**

Don Domanski presently lives in Wolfville, Nova Scotia.

CHILDHOOD MEMORY

my mother cracked open
a family story
and the tea was poured again.

while all along
the hills of the moon
I heard the tale retold

I heard the distance claim it
and saw us all fall dead.

Don Domanski

A MINER WRITES A POEM

I

what exhausts you
is all this light
the cool whites
and brilliant blues

heaven is black
and clear as a tunnel

this bright sun
is your sort of thing
lion-yellow
squelching the rock-face
to a silent frown
that I never get used to

even in the earth's gut
the sea drips in
tamping the colourless pit
to get a response

II

a black colliery
sits on my left shoulder
its mottled eye
is never mute

a black head
against a black sky
mimicking my voice
and flapping its wings

blackness is something
you could use
a favourite tool
a good flower

blooming in the eye.

Don Domanski

RETURNING TO SYDNEY

I stood in the doorway
entire evergreens were on my side
entire geraniums
who always seem to know my desires
desires which are always the weight
of a single owl burnt to a fine ash

I stood in the doorway
with a thin covering of algae
along my hand
the hand of rainy days
bouquet of fingers
turning the brass knob
of a starling
(a bestial growl)

I stood in the doorway
the tears in my pocket
purring softly to themselves
as the moon rose high
above the brown wooden house
where a bottletop lay
beneath a chair
in which someone sat waiting
for me all night long.

Don Domanski

DESERTED FARMHOUSE
(Coxheath Cape Breton)

after the meltage of years nothing stands
but a half-chair and solid roof
for a dead Mrs.

nothing but her tonnage
her absolute ownership
of the few floorboards
and remaining light

the bent fork in the corner
once handled every day
is now a door

these nails and beams
are also her occult
her way back

looking beyond my face
she views a different yard
with smaller trees
and someone doing something
very ordinary and exciting.

Don Domanski

Clive Doucet / Grand Etang

Clive Doucet was born in London, England in 1946, the son of a war bride who soon followed her RCAF husband to Nova Scotia. The family eventually found its way back to Grand Etang where Clive's father had grown up. Doucet now lives in Ottawa where he works for the Department of Indian Affairs and Northern Development as a speech writer for the minister.

His novel, **Disneyland Please,** was nominated for the **Books in Canada** First Novel Award in 1979. A second novel, **John Coe's War** was published in 1983. Along with plays, poetry and television scripts, Doucet has published a lively memoir called, My Grandfather's Cape Breton. "Stan Goes to the Doctor" is an excerpt from a forthcoming novel.

I don't remember being poor in Antigonish or Grand Etang. I think this was because we had a lot of relatives there. I have the impression that when you are small, a lot of relatives make up for not having sofas and armchairs.

Grant Etang is the village of my father and his father. It is a hometown of the mind and heart. For no matter how much it changes or I change, Grand Etang will still be my hometown, which is what I believe hometowns are all about. They are your primary references.

Stan Goes to the Doctor

by Clive Doucet

The waiting room was crowded and hot with expectant mothers. Their bellies and breasts rounded out like helium balloons. Expectant mothers and tough looking professional women - 'trendy" was the word that came to mind. Trendy and capable. The women in the waiting room were all fashionable. They did not look exploited or downtrodden. They looked tough and ready to bark 'male chauvinist pig'. The babies in their bellies felt the same way.

Stan Philips shifted in his chair uncomfortably. He was the only male in the waiting room. The women ignored him. They were all reading *National Geographic* or *Business Weekly*. They were not sweating. They were not nervous. They did not need men, or when they did, they were ordered up. The babies in their bellies came from wise decisions based on the need to sneeze between the legs.

They hadn't even noticed a male chauvinist pig was in their waiting room. Stan Philips had noticed; his large feet tenderly clad in heavy, brown brogues splayed out over the waiting room floor. They looked messy. His legs refused to stay still, alternately bunching up under the chair and lengthening out. Lengthened out, they took up an unfair proportion of the small room. Bunched up, Stan felt uncomfortable. The trousers buckled behind the knee and around the crotch. Stan felt the sick feeling return, his head becoming alarmingly dizzy. He focused on the Isle of Sky. It said 'Scott's Drugs' under the Isle of Sky and then 'July'. The pain in his belly eased as he gazed on the Isle of Sky.

"Stan Philips," called the receptionist. Stan raised his hand and then stood. She pointed down the hall with her pencil. *Male*

Chauvinist Pig, cried the born and the unborn. Stan followed the direction indicated. It led to a small examination room off Dr. Cameron's office. The receptionist came up behind him and opened the door. "Strip to your underwear, please." Stan nodded and waited for the blonde head to disappear. He wasn't going to disrobe with the flashlight eyes of the receptionist on him. She smiled and disappeared.

Stan undressed as quickly as he could, fumbling with his trousers as he did so. In his haste, his foot caught in the trouser leg. He wobbled and then slowly crashed to the floor. The door opened and Dr. Cameron entered. She was even more stunning than the receptionist. Her legs arching up underneath a demure beige dress. Stan averted his eyes, his breath coming in small, painful gasps.

"I fell," he said lamely. Dr. Cameron nodded and walked over to a small desk where her equipment was laid out.

"You're here for a medical?"

"No, well, sort of." Dr. Cameron turned the full power of her baby-blue eyes on him. He felt the colour rise in his face.

"I have a pain," said Stan.

"Where?"

"Here," he said, pointing to his middle.

"Lie down, will you please? On your back."

"Yes," replied Stan unnecessarily. He lay down on the examining table. In spite of the cold, he felt himself break out into a dense, smelly sweat. What if he should get a hard-on? What if she should laugh? He felt her hands trace firmly over his abdomen, then higher up across his stomach.

"Where does it hurt?"

"Here," said Stan, drawing a straight line across the top of his stomach.

"When you take a deep breath, does it feel like something is going to tear?"

"Exactly," replied Stan, astonished that she could describe the pain so accurately.

"Any other symptoms?"

"I can't seem to get a deep breath; I start to pant. I can't sleep at night. I get terrible heartburn. Out of keeping with what I eat. Two days ago, I fainted in the street." The parade of miseries poured out of Stan's mouth before he could stop it. He hadn't meant to say anything about the heartburn. Only old people were supposed to get heartburn.

Dr. Cameron nodded and went back to her desk. She jotted something down on a sheet of paper. "You may sit up." She said this casually as she pulled out a very large syringe. It looked like a needle for a horse.

"You're kidding," smiled Stan, trying to stay calm, his skin prickling with fear. Needles of any kind terrified him. This one seemed right out of a nightmare. "You're going to put that in my arm?"

"No, your diaphragm."

"My diaphragm?"

"Yes, where the pain is."

"Can't you give me a pill?"

"That would be like killing a mosquito with a steam shovel," said Dr. Cameron, pulling a solution of some liquid into the syringe.

"What's the matter with me?"

"Your diaphragm has seized up."

Stan looked uncomprehendingly into Dr. Cameron's baby-blue eyes.

"The diaphragm is a long, flat organ. It helps you breath by expanding or contracting. You've been so tense that the muscles have squeezed it and squeezed it until it is no longer expanding properly. That's why you can't get a deep breath. That's also why you're getting the tearing pain and the heartburn." Dr. Cameron smiled confidently.

"You seem very sure."

"You would be surprised at how many guys get this complaint."

"Don't you get it from women?"

"No."

"What's in the needle?" Stan asked, trying to play for time as she advanced towards him.

"Cortesone. We don't know how it works but it works. Put your hands behind your back like this. Clasp them" Stan did as he was told, his belly immediately naked to the needle. "Don't hunch," said Dr. Cameron as she swabbed some disinfectant over his stomach. Then deftly, cunningly, she inserted the horse needle into his belly. It sunk in and in. Stan braced himself for intense, incredible pain, but he felt nothing except an agreeable popping sensation, like champagne rising in a glass. Suddenly, he could breath. Deep, regular breaths. There was no tearing feeling under his heart.

"Like magic, isn't it?" said Dr. Cameron.

"Yes, like magic," he repeated, feeling a great rush of relief and gratitude towards the doctor. He wanted to invite her out immediately to the nearest expensive restaurant for a long, intimate tete-a-tete, and from there to the nearest bed.

"You're probably constipated too," said Dr. Cameron, matter of factly.

"Yes," Stan admitted miserably, "and I'm a virgin." The words came out and hung there in the still air between them. Who had said that, wondered Stan. Had he said it? The notion was horrifying.

Dr. Cameron calmly took apart the syringe and began cleaning it. "You should be proud. I didn't know there were any left."

"It's not funny. I'm 21, almost 22 years old."

"Careful, you're hyperventilating."

Stan Philips sat down on the little white stool. He was so miserable that he felt like crying.

"Aren't you going to get dressed?" There was no response. "Twenty-one and a virgin is not the end of the world."

"Everyone I know got laid in first-year university."

"Do you have some medical problem?"

"Not that I know of. Sometimes I wish that I did ," he sighed, feeling some calm return.

"Constipation you can fix with diet and exercise. My nurse will give you a sheet. The other I can do nothing about. It's outside my area of expertise." Dr. Cameron smiled in a way that belied this statement. Stan felt his stomach tighten and his heart begin to pound.

"What happens if I get it again?" asked Stan, feeling his stomach.

"Come back for more cortesone."

"You have no mercy," sighed Stan almost to himself, but she heard him. The boy was beginning to irritate her.

"Would you complain to a male doctor that you were a virgin?"

"I don't know. No, I guess not."

"Then why complain to me?"

"It's been on my mind . . . I thought you might have some

advice."

Dr. Cameron shrugged. Her lower lip pouting a fraction of an inch. "I understand celibacy does not have the prestige that it once had, but on the other hand sex is highly over-rated."

"I'd like to try it before I made a judgment."

This brought a small smile to the handsome lips of Dr. Cameron. "My advice is to relax and the inevitable will occur."

"I can't relax until the inevitable happens."

"Catch 22."

"Exactly," said Stan, for the first time sensing the doctor was seeing him as a person instead of a bundle of symptoms.

"Rape is not the alternative."

"I realize that."

"Are you sure?"

Stan looked up at her from his position on the footstool, amazed. "I won't dignify that question with a response."

Doctor Cameron looked down at Stan Philips sitting in his underwear on her footstool. They both began to smile. Dr. Cameron walked towards the door. "If you have more trouble with your diaphragm, come back. In the meantime, I'd try and find some way to dissipate your energies. Perhaps a sport of some kind. One that didn't have women around." She smiled and left Stan to contemplate his bare feet. They were long and white and unexercised. They looked vulnerable. In fact, Stan Philips looked vulnerable all over. He stood up in front of the mirror. Like his feet, his body had an unused look. The face long and lineless. The hair parted and combed in an innocuous way. He could be a student, a businessman, an anything. Just print in the label below the photo that said Stan Philips. The shoulders were simply attachments for his arms. His chest melting into his stomach. There were no lines around his muscles. No parts of his body which bulged or sagged. No interesting lines in his face. His body had not been used. That's what Stan's reflection said to him.

The door swung open. It was the receptionist. "Could you dress a little faster, Mr. Philips. I have another patient waiting." She smiled professionally and shut the door.

Stan Philips began to pull on his trousers. For the first time in months, he had no pain below his heart. He bent with no effort. There was no dizzy sensation. Sureness, a calmness began to settle in his mind. The moment would happen. He would meet a girl and suddenly it would just be evident. She would look at him and they would know, the time had come. It would be perfect and they would drift on a timeless sea.

Stan Philips laced up his brogues and left the examining room. He did not stop for the sheet on diet and exercise. He walked right past the pregnant ladies, right past the *National Geographics* right past the *Business Weekly,* right past the coat rack, right out into the hall.

Destiny awaited.

Donna Doyle / Rocky Bay

Donna Doyle was born at Gannon Road just outside North Sydney. She graduated with a Home Economics Certificate from the Nova Scotia Teachers College in Truro and taught school in Arichat and North Sydney. After she married, she and her husband moved into the Doyle family homestead in Rocky Bay.

"The Feast of Christ the King" first appeared in **The Pottersfield Portfolio, Volume 4.** She has also received an award for her non-fiction from the Writers' Federation of Nova Scotia.

> *Growing up on Gannon Road, I spent most of my summer days playing in the woods, building with spruce boughs, jumping trees, catching polywogs in the pond, picking blueberries, cherries and chestnuts, endlessly watching the trains wondering who they were taking to where. I went to a two-room schoolhouse complete with pot-bellied stove and outhouse. At night I would be closing my eyes as the William Carson, the ferry to Newfoundland blew its whistle and the trains shunted at the station.*
>
> *My grandparents' home in Iona was a different world. We crossed the ferry at Grand Narrows and entered a place where they spoke Gaelic, sang Gaelic songs and stepdanced. They ran a farm with cows, horses, pigs, sheep and chickens. Meals were a feast of homemade butter, cheese, bread, cream, fresh meat, garden vegetables. Afterwards we listened to endless tales of the supernatural, forerunners, spirits, miracles and magic cures.*
>
> *If Cape Breton sounds like Fantasy Island, it is not. No one knows the feel of reality like a Cape Bretoner. Years of unemployment or threatened unemployment have made them a careful people, a humble people. The jobs they have may be miles away from home, beneath the ocean floor, or on the fickle Atlantic but they are eager to work wherever or at whatever they can. Cape Bretoners are more concerned with what they are than with what they have.*

The Feast of Christ the King

by Donna Doyle

It was the feast of Christ the King and we gathered to celebrate as others had done so many years before. The dusty school basement which Sister Dominica insisted we call the auditorium, was decorated for the occasion. Grade after grade filled in and stood in orderly fashion, row by row in the center of the room. The teachers took their proper places against the far wall. Sister Dominica strode to the speaker's platform.

I stared from the fifth grade row. We were here to praise Christ but my worship was all for Sister Dominica. She was the school principal, the choir leader and my idol. Although only five feet tall, she had the commanding presence of one destined to lead. One look from those piercing blue eyes and her will was done.

Sister Dominica had the face of an angel, as finely formed as the tiny porcelain figurines which graced her desk. Her habit was as neat and as exact as her demands. I dreamed of one day being just like her. I would wait after school to run errands for her. If I was lucky she'd let me carry her bag to the car. Usually, she'd sit at her desk and listen to Mantovani records until her car arrived. There was the magic of an unknown world about her. I would stand at the back of the room trying to study my catechism so that she would choose me to teach the younger grades, but mostly, I studied Sister Dominica.

Today I was ready, just in case she asked questions about the feast of Christ the King. I knew it was when Jesus was brought before Pilate. Pilate falsely accused Jesus of many crimes, the final one being, "You say that you are a king!" Jesus did not even try to answer the charges and He was crucified. I knew the reading by heart. "Worthy the Lamb who is brought to the slaughter."

I hoped she asked me.

Sister Dominica began the reading in the strong, vibrant voice the good Lord had given her. "Worthy the Lamb . . ."

A hush fell over the room as Diane Waters tiptoed into her place in line. In a flurry of swinging beads and rustling habit, Sister Dominica flew from the stage. She gripped Diane's shoulder and pulled her into the aisle.

"What is the meaning of this disgusting show?" she thundered.

Diane made no reply.

Diane was wearing slacks. Girls were never allowed to wear slacks to school. If the weather was cold you could wear slacks under a skirt until you got inside the school, but the slacks were removed before you entered the class. Diane had broken the rule.

"So you think you're too big for my rules. You want to parade yourself in front of the boys in those wicked pants. Parade!"

Sister Dominica shoved Diane to the front of the room. Diane stood there, head bent, her tiny body trembling, trying desperately to hold back the tears.

"Go on, march up and down every aisle and let's see what your classmates think of your appearance."

Diane stumbled past each row. When she came to mine I couldn't bear to look at her. She was my friend; she was decent and shy. I wished she would say something. I wished it would be over soon.

"Pants are for girls who walk streets, Miss Waters. Pants are disgusting and vulgar. You are disgusting and vulgar. You are not fit company for decent children. Isn't she disgusting, children?"

"Yes, Sister Dominica." I heard my voice with the others. I felt sick to my stomach.

Diane completed her walk and tried to return to her place in line.

"You're not finished yet, tramp!" yelled Sister Dominica as she led Diane to the teachers' line.

"Have a good look, teachers, at this filthy girl. Look at her pants, look at the holes in them. She is a disgrace."

Sister Dominica would not tolerate anyone who displayed their poverty so shamelessly. Diane walked slowly past each teacher. They knew her only crime was that of having poor parents and living the farthest away from the school. Unlike Sister Dominica, Diane walked to school each day no matter how cold she felt.

The teachers looked at the rags Diane wore. They knew their own children would not leave the house in such dress. They saw a humble and courageous girl. They looked at Diane and were ashamed, but the shame was their own.

Diane's body shook as she wiped her eyes on her sweater sleeve. Still silent, she crept back into line.

Sister Dominica, recharged as if she'd just conquered Satan himself, mounted the platform and began the reading again. This time I didn't watch.

"Worthy the Lamb who is brought to the slaughter."

It was the feast of Christ the King and we gathered to celebrate as others had done so many years before.

Rita Joe / Eskasoni

Rita Joe was born in Whycocomagh in 1932. Her mother died in 1937 and her father died in 1942. When she was twelve years old, she went to the Shubenacadie Residential School and later worked at the Halifax Infirmary. In 1952 Rita Joe moved to Boston where she worked as a hospital attendant, an elevator operator and a factory worker. There she met and married Frank Joe who was also a Cape Bretoner.

Rita Joe and her husband returned to Cape Breton to live at Eskasoni where they have remained for over 25 years. She has eight children.

In the 1960s she began publishing articles in **Micmac News** and soon after began writing poetry. Abanaki Press collected her verse in **The Poems of Rita Joe,** published in 1978. Her work has appeared in a number of anthologies.

The Cape Breton that I love has only to be seen to be appreciated. The people, like the island are colourful and easy to get along with.

In writing, a gentle approach has always been my way because, in 50 years of my life, I have noticed that nothing else has worked more positively.

There is a hill, a watching place
Where we see the rivers entering Bras D'Or.
That is where we float on still waters
Rafts made of spruce
With suspended scalloped shells
Waiting for spatfall.

With expectation we wait
For the spark of life to cling,
In the warm waters of Bras D'Or,
To the shells hanging by wire
On pontoons of spruce.
We wait for spatfall.

There is a hill, a watching place
From where we see our labours
Scattered on the waters
With bobbing buoys, a marking place
Of pontoons of spruce.
We wait for spatfall.

We are the Mi'Kmaw
As old as the sea.
With expectation of advancement
We foster nature,
Farming oysters
Around the fiords, near where we live.

Rita Joe

Images from the past—
Of the man in the bush.
Wekayi in mind
To alter the picture.

You see me as I am,
A conquered master of this land;
I see myself the same,
But still I fight.

Otium cum dignitate.
So shall we,
A people least thought of,
Attain grace.

Rita Joe

From the fountain the patterns fall
Cascading the being
Holding the soul.
The seed alleviates and softens
Scaling the burden.

How marvelous!
Dealing with sight,
To soar above the bounds
Of yesterday's fight.
The noble is precious now
How dear the culture.
I did not see the time that was
Or today,
But now I flow and murmur
Calling to attention.

Rita Joe

I

They say that I must live
a white man's way.
This day and age
Still being bent to what they say,
My heart remains
Tuned to native time.

I must dress conservative in style
And have factory shoes upon my feet.
Leave the ways they say
Are wild.
Forfeit a heritage
That is conquered.

I must accept what this century
Has destroyed and left behind —
The innocence of my ancestry.

I must forget father sky
And mother earth,
And hurt his land we love
With towering concrete.

II

If I must fight
Their war as well
Or share in conquests
And slip away in drink or drugs,
All wished for wealth
Is mockery to me.

My body yields, wanting luxuries,
But my heart reverts
To so-called savagery.

If we are slow
Embracing today's thoughts,
Be patient with us awhile.
Seeing
What wrongs have been wrought,
Native ways seem not so wild.

Rita Joe

John E.C. MacDonald . Sydney Mines

John E.C. MacDonald was born in New Glasgow, raised and educated in Truro, then returned to New Glasgow to work as a clerk in an auto supply store for seven dollars a week. His income resulted in the purchase of his first typewriter on which he wrote endless letters that drove his relatives crazy. He went to work for the railroad in 1949, moved to Cape Breton a year later, and has remained there ever since.

"Junk" first appeared in **Volume 2** of **The Pottersfield Portfolio** in 1980.

> *My "insight" into the life on Cape Breton ain't so simple a matter to discuss. I do know that if you're hungry down here, y' get fed. If you're cold, somebody'll give you a coat. And if y' need a punch in the mouth, you'll get that, too, as quickly and generously as anything else y'might need if you're not too proud to ask for it.*
>
> *Pride — that, I think, is the thing about Cape Bretoners.*
>
> *Times are changing rapidly everywhere else, but not rapidly enough down here. The pride I mentioned can't do much good when old ways of life, and the people who lived them, are being pried out by new and inevitable technologies.*
>
> *I don't know what we're to do about it . . . but I do suspect that there's enough of that devilish streak left amongst us, somewhere, to keep us from becoming nothing more'n a bunch of old fogies in Senior Citizens' Homes and an even larger bunch of good-for-nothing young bastards in community jails, with an even larger bunch of greedy politicians romping about in between, gathering up government grants and royal commissionings like posies . . . .! Somehow or other we'll get bridges built between what was good of the old and what'll be good of the new; we'll get our young people back and some more besides — and, godammit! — we'll make proper Cape Bretoners of the lot of them!*

Junk

by John E.C. MacDonald

Shivering, Jean Tellet poked furiously at ash and cinders in the ancient coal range until she bared the grates. Cursing the cold, cursing George who snored away in the other room, cursing everything in sight, she plummetted about the shabby, chilly room like a maddened gannet, picking up trash from last night's party for kindling.

"Damn them!" she snarled, snatching an empty beer carton from under the table. "Goddam them all, the boozin' bastards!" The ragged hem of her faded green nightgown tangled in the heels of her filthy fur slippers, ripped some more. She yanked it free, and grabbed a clawful of empty cigarette packages, an empty egg carton, some pages of yesterday's newspaper. "The boozin' good for nothing sonsawhores! They coulda kept the fire on!" She spied another beer carton behind a chair, swooped upon it, kicked it. It spun, end around end, over the stained and buckled linoleum toward the stove. From the dish and bottle strewn table, she added a couple of crackling cookie packages to her armload. Spilled sugar, crusts and crumbs crunched under her feet.

Somebody's left an inch of rum in an uncapped pint at the back of the table. With a growl, she grabbed it, downed it, grimaced.

Dirty, gummed-up, fire-blackened pots and pans cluttered the back of the stove. With a sweep of her arm she swept them clattering to the floor. A groan of protest came from the other room. "Ach. Go to hell!" she hissed, replacing the pots and pans with her load of trash.

The room's chill caught up to her, climbed her legs. Her knees shook and her thighs flinched. As fast as she could make her fingers work, she ripped and tore and crushed and crammed the stove with cardboard and paper. She found matches. The first one broke. The second smothered itself. The third one caught. Flames roared up the flue.

Jesus Lord Christ - only an inch or two of dust left in the coal scuttle. Damn George! "Arrrrgh . . .!" she yelled toward the bedroom door. She dumped the duff into the fire, snatched a tattered black sweatercoat off a hook beside the stove, put it on, fastened it tight about her with safety pins. She scooted, bucket and shovel rattling, to the front door, went out.

The two-roomed, sway-backed shack looked like it had been dumped with all the other junk - wrecked cars, broken washing machines and refrigerators and stoves and upside-down baby carriages - in the middle of the bog-ridden field, here on the backside of town. A rutted lane originated in front of the place, ascended unsteadily toward a paved street where rigid, high windows of more respectable homes stared, stiffly sneering at her as she darted across the yard.

"T'hell with yez!" she spat at them, bending to the coal pile, gasping and grunting each time her shovel struck. "T'hell with yez all!" April sunlight, new risen and unripened, cracked glints off chrome edged rusted hulks, off the mass of bobby pins that fastened thin, colorless hair to her bony birdlike skull. Quickly, she filled the bucket, hobbled back into the house, bucket bumping against her knees. Damn. It was warmer out than it was in! She kicked the door shut behind her.

The duff, for once, had caught well. Another fistfull of trash and a bit of poking, and she had the fire going good. She made a noisy business of adding more coal, of filling up the teakettle at the single sink tap and slamming it on the stove to heat. She ran to the toilet in the stinky cubby between the rooms. Thank Christ she had taken off the seat (its bolts had broken long ago) and stood it in the corner before she went to bed last night; George or somebody had puked all over the bowl. She replaced the seat, hoisted up her skirts, and went. Jesus the place was cold . . .

She was holding out her scrawny arms to be warmed in the steadily rising heat from the stove when George hollered. She sighed, shook her head. Oh, that heat felt good!

George hollered again.

"Whaddya want?" she yelled back, turning her arms in the

warmth.

She couldn't make out what George said next. Couldn't make him out half the time, anyway, him with his tobacco chewer's toothless mouth. He gummed his words same way he gummed most of his food. Coulda had teeth years ago, stupid bugger, if only he'd gone and got them. Lots of money, the old days, before he started boozin' every paynight with that pack of bums. Now, he didn't give a damn. Hmph - neither did she!

He hollered again.

Folding her arms and humping her sweater tight about her, she went to the bedroom door. "Whaddya want?" she said.

George, everything on but his boots, lay lumped on his side, top blanket only half covering him. She had a sheet and a pillowcase, her side of the bed; George was drooling all over them. Two steps and a snatch, she had them off the bed and flung onto the bleary-mirrored dresser.

"What time is it . . .?" George mumbled, his rheumy eyes trying to focus on her from the old sofa cushion he used as a pillow.

"It's after seven o'clock," she told him. "Why . . .?"

"Gotta go to work."

"Y'don't work today. It's Saturday."

"Gotta get up . . ."

"Y'don't gotta get up. Christ Almighty, y'only went t'bed three, four hours ago!"

"Mrrrmph . . ." In a moment, he was snoring again, both hands folded under his cheek. A hole in the drawn, crazy-cracked window shade behind him let in a ray of sunlight that fell in the thick tangle of hair just above his ear. Jean gazed at him a minute, remembering when that hair had been sleek and black and well cut and the face under it had been clean and full-jawed and . . . ach! She went back to the other room.

The kettle was getting hot. Amongst the mess on the table she found a mug that was half clean. She took it to the sink and rinsed it out. Amid the junk on the cupboard she found the bottle of instant coffee. Behind an empty wine bottle she found the sugar bowl. She made herself a cup of coffee.

An old wringer type washer with three legs and a stack of bricks to hold it up stood in the corner at the right of the stove. The thing didn't work, but it sure held a lot of dirty clothes she had nowhere else to put. When it got too full, Jean stuffed a green garbage bag with as much as she could carry and went uptown to the laundromat with it. It was too full now. Some of the stink in the musty old shack came from it. But other things could come from that old washer too . . .

With a quick check on the bedroom doorway, Jean raised the washer's battered lid and rummaged deep inside. She yanked out a full quart of rum. Chortling, she opened it, spilled a hefty dollop into her coffee. She drank a good swig straight from the bottle before she put it back.

"Hawwww . . ." she chuckled to herself, picking up the mug for a belly-warming draught. "Them buggers woulda wet their pants if they knew I had that, and two more, in there last night." Ten bucks or so she'd make on each, next week, when George was outta the house and she could peddle it, a shot at a time, to the bums who came salvaging whatever junk they could scrounge from the field, outside. Kept herself in booze, this little dido. That's why she didn't mind the furtive pickup trucks that snuck down from uptown to dump junk they couldn't be bothered hauling way over to the landfill place. George, himself, coulda made a nice little bit, whacking that stuff apart and selling it to the junk dealers. But nahhh, George had a job.

Some jeezeless job! - beltin' coal around for 95 dollars a week, up at the chutes, comin' home dirty and goin' back just as dirty. They'd doused him once, up there, with a firehose. Said he was lousy and pollutin' the place. Told him not to come back until he changed his clothes and had a bath. A bath in this place . . .? Haw!

He didn't even have a change of clothes until she went up and bought them for him. That was some week, that was. Guys that had doused him took up a collection and brought the money down to her. Two hundred and twelve dollars. When the guy that brought it saw inside the house, he chucked in another twenty of his own. God, the gawpmouth look on his face . . .

There'd been enough money left over for an outfit for herself, but George beat it out of her and went off with his boozin' buddies for a whole week, damn him . . .

She reached into the washer, poured herself another drink, gulped it down straight. She began the business of clearing up.

George woke up again, an hour or so later. He stumbled to the toilet, stumbled out again, yanking at his zipper. Jean had changed her clothes, gone out for another bucket of coal.

Another dollop or two from her bottle hadn't hurt her a bit. She'd stayed out for awhile, enjoying a smoke while watching a blond young man in blue jeans and a bomber jacket prowling for parts around a wrecked Plymouth at the farthest end of the field.

She had warm slacks on, brown ones she'd found in one of the old cars herself. Some kind of muck that wouldn't wash out had been spilled down one leg of them, but they had a nice built-in crease and they fit her good. Above the slacks she wore the thick grey turtleneck she'd bought for a dollar at that new-to-you place uptown, and over that the white nylon jacket somebody'd given George to take home. Her head still gleamed with bobby pins; she had taken the time to rearrange them a bit. Her head always shone with bobby pins. Cards of bobby pins were the only jewellery she had.

On her feet were a pair of brown rubber boots lined with some kind of fuzz that felt pretty good. They were boy's boots, but what the hell was the difference. She'd got them out of one of the old cars too. Two years, she'd had them. Two years. Two Springs like this . . . two more years of living off other people's trash . . . fifty-three years altogether of nothin' good ever happening to her . . .

But what the hell . . .

She swung up the coal bucket, heaved it into the house. George was standing by the sink, watching her come in. His pants were twisted. One toe poked out of a hole in his work socks. Buttons had come off his workshirt overnight and grey wool underwear showed through the gaps. Hair tufted like winter grass tangled in all directions on his head. His eyes, red and watery, squinted from cheeks mottled permanently by dirt and coal dust; the eternal dribble of tobacco juice stained the corners of his toothless mouth.
"Where y'been . . .? he said.

"I been out gettin' coal," she said, thumping the bucket down behind him, beside the stove. Christ, he stank. Always he stank . . of rum, of perspiration, of dirty drawers. But Saturday mornings he stank worse than ever - of spilled booze, of puke, and piss down his pants when he missed the toilet like he always did during his Friday night drunks.

"Take them clothes off you today," she said. "I'm gonna be doin' a wash, after a while. Y'want, I'll heat some water for a bath."

"Frig the bath . . .!" he mumbled. "Where's that rum . . .?"

"That rum I left on the table last night. Just enough t'get me goin' this mornin'."

"Where were y'gonna get any more . . .?"

"I got money."

"I didn't see no rum."

"Yes y'did! I can smell it offa ya."

"Shit in yer hat!" she told him, bending to fill the coal shovel.

He kicked her, sent her sprawling over the coal bucket. The coal bucket upset, spilling her and coal onto the floor. She screeched, struggled to sit up.

"Look what y'did. The only clean clothes I got." Sitting, she brushed at her sweater. Standing up, she brushed at her slacks.

"Gimme something to eat," he ordered.

"You'll burn in hell before I'll get you anything t'eat this day." She righted the coal bucket, hunkered down to use her hand and the shovel to scrape up the spillage. His foot flicked out to kick her again. She twisted. His foot missed. With all her might, and before he could avoid it, she swung the shovel. It caught him full on the ankle. He yowled, writhed in anguish.

"Lord jumpin' Christ, y'broke it, y'broke it, y'broke it!" he howled, clutching his ankle, wincing with pain.

"Too damn bad if I didn't," she said, shovelling coal into the fire. She went to the sink to wash her hands, then wiped at her clothes with the sour sinkcloth, scowling.

"Cook me an egg," he groaned, still writhing and clutching his ankle.

"You and them damn fools ate all the eggs and just about everything else in the house last night."

"Gimme some cornflakes."

"We got no cornflakes."

"Gimme something then, godammit."

"We got baloney and bread, is all. You got money, I'll go up to the store, after . . ."

He said nothing.

She dug the frying pan out of the sink, slammed it onto the stove. The first piece of cloth her searching eyes saw was a pair of his shorts dangling out of the washing machine. Her rummaging earlier, must've stirred them up from the bottom; it had been September, October maybe, last time she'd emptied the thing.

He wouldn't be wearing shorts again until the middle of May. She grabbed them and wiped the pan clean. "Hmph," she snorted to herself. "A little more brown won't hurt them."

George was staring at her, goggle-eyed. "What'd I just see you doin . . . ?" he said.

She took the packet of boloney from the refrigerator, nicked her finger on the broken handle as she usually did. "Damn," she said, sucking at the scratch. "You gotta tape that handle up, one of these days." She peeled back plastic, stripped off rind. She fired slices of boloney into the pan.

"You filthy bitch!" George roared. He leaped to his feet. His ankle still hurt. He limped to the stove. He sent her flying with one sweep of his arm, sent the frying pan flying with another. Jean landed, wailing, against the wall. The frying pan sailed across the room, crashed through the window behind the table. Plastic curtains, ripped off their hooks, fluttered out after it. A hem, torn away by a shard of glass, stuck there, fluttering. George and Jean stood stunned for a minute, then they both started yelling.

"Y'crazy idiot, look what y' —"

"Don't call me names like that, George. Don't you ever —"

"I'll call you any friggin' name I want."

"No y'won't, damn you." She grabbed the boiling teakettle off the stove, heaved it at him. It missed him by a yard, but the water that gushed out of it when it hit the floor sped across the linoleum, soaked his thickly stockinged feet.

Howling and stomping with rage and agony, he snatched the poker off the stove and flailed at her with it. She ducked, but the hooked tip caught in her bobby pins. He yanked. She screeched. The pins came loose. She fled, screaming, to the other end of the room. There was an ancient, skin-burst stuffed chair in the corner. She got behind it.

He came after her, wet feet sloshing. He didn't see the slice of boloney that had been flung that far. Down he went, yowling. His nose struck the edge of the thing she called a coffee table and began to bleed profusely. He stared, drop-jawed, at the bubbled blood on his hands and between his fingers. He scrambled to his feet, blood splattering off his chin. "I'll kill ya. I'll kill ya!" he screamed.

Throwing the poker aside, he lunged at the chair, pinned her into the corner with it. He leaped into the seat, started cuffing and slapping and punching her. She wrapped her arms around her head and dodged and ducked and screamed and screamed and screamed. Blood from George's nose dripped and runnelled all over her.

The blond young man in blue jeans and the bomber jacket, from the field, burst through the front door, thundered into the room.

"What the Christ is goin' . . . Jesus!" He strode over, grabbed George by the waist, hauled him away from her.

The young man felt warm blood on his hands, looked, dropped George in the middle of the floor. George, on his hands and knees, scrambled back toward the chair. The young man grabbed him again, hauled him back. He was pretty strong, but George was strong, too. He clubbed the young man on the knee with his bloody fist and made for the chair again. Jean had sunk down behind it and was sobbing and moaning in the corner.

The young man, angry himself, now, grabbed George brutally by the hair of his head and dragged him, squealing with pain and rage, to a chair by the broken window. "Sit!" he commanded.

George sat, burbling and snuffling and gasping. "I'll kill her! I'll kill her! I'll kill her!"

"You'll leave her alone or I'll break your goddam neck," the young man said. He hauled off and struck George violently on the meat of his ear with his open palm.

George yowled, put his blood-smeared face into his blood-smeared hands, and began to weep.

The young man went to the corner, pulled away the chair. Jean, head on her knees, was sitting on the floor, crying. "You hurt . . .?" the young man said.

She stopped crying, fisted her eyes. She saw his big yellow boots looked up. "N-n-no . . ." she said. Her arms would be black and blue for a month and she'd taken a crack on the jaw that was sore, but she wasn't hurt.

"You got a phone . . .?" the young man asked.

"Phone . . .?"

"Yeah, phone. I'm gonna call the cops. That guy should be put away."

"Put away . . .?"

"Yeah, put away. That guy coulda killed you. Nobody should

have t'put up with that." He looked around at the squalid room the decrepit furniture, the bare-legged sink, the splay-footed refrigerator, the battered stove, the uneven, sinking floor, the sagging walls, the bellied ceiling. He smelled the stink of mould and rot and piss-riddled wood. He saw the smashed window with the rag of curtain fluttering. He saw George shuddering in ugly misery amid a pool of shattered glass. He felt the chill of the breeze flowing through the door behind him. "Nobody should have t'put up with this," he said.

Jean brushed at her clothes. "You look like a nice young man," she said. "What's your name?"

He told her his name.

"Oh. Your dad works for the railway, eh? I know him. I went on the train, once . . ." She picked a fluff of dust off her sweater. "No, we don't have a phone."

"I'll call from another house, then. That man's nuts. He should be put away. He'll hurt you bad one of these days."

"Naw, he's not crazy. Don't bother with the cops. Thirty years, he never really hurt me yet . . ."

The young man looked at her. "Thirty years . . .? Christ!"

"Okay . . .?" she said, managing a smile for him.

"Well . . . yeah, then, okay, if that's what you want . . ." Frowning, the young man left.

Jean went to the sink, filled a plastic bowl with water. She dug a fairly clean towel out of the washer, pulled up a chair beside George's at the table. The bleeding had stopped.

Carefully, she began to wipe his face. "Poor ol' fella . . ." she crooned, while he watched her. "We're already 'put away', both of us, ain't we . . ."

Hugh MacLennan / Glace Bay

Hugh MacLennan was born in Glace Bay in 1907. After attending Dalhousie University, he won a Rhodes scholarship to Oxford and later completed classical studies at Princeton. Since 1951 he has taught English at McGill University in Montreal.

MacLennan's first novel was published in 1941 and he went on to receive five Governor General's Awards. Among his well-known works of fiction are: **Barometer Rising, Two Solitudes, The Precipice, The Watch that Ends the Night**, and **Return of the Sphinx.** His most recent novel, **Voices in Time,** appeared in 1980.

Each Man's Son, MacLennan's fourth novel, was published by MacMillan in 1951. The setting is a coal mining community on Cape Breton in 1913. In the words of the critic, George Woodcock, it is the story of "the last days of a rather childish and fundamentally well-intentioned primitive who has become involved and finally broken by the corrupt and destroying world of commercialized brutality which centres on the boxing ring." The novel goes much deeper as well, focussing on the cultural, economic and social struggles within a Cape Breton coal town. "I have used my native island as background for a story because I love it," MacLennan states, "and also because the emotions and experiences could have been true of people living anywhere at any time."

> *It was a place, I used to assume, where more people were born than died. Ambitious men tended to leave it; having done so, they also tended to yearn for it and to save up to come home on vacations. Wherever they went, they had the habit of telling strangers it was one of the loveliest spots on earth.*

Each Man's Son: Chapter Two

by Hugh MacLennan

Downstairs the late light of evening was in the little parlor when Mollie pushed open the door. It was a room they had seldom used when Archie was home, but he had been away four years now and she had turned it into a workroom. In the center of the floor was a frame with a partially finished rug mounted on it and a debris of materials on the floor where she could put her hands on them as she worked. Against one wall stood a dresser with her best china displayed on its smooth top. In front of the window stood a solid table holding a glass lamp. Two rocking chairs, which Mollie now skirted in order to look at herself in the mirror that hung over the open coal grate, filled the room. There was one other piece of furniture in the corner, a tall whatnot reaching three quarters of the way to the ceiling.

She was touching a piece of chamois to her nose when she heard the grinding of wheels and knew the streetcar had cleared the bridge. Quickly she put on her hat and left the house, but when she reached the sidewalk she saw the tram as it stopped at the corner seventy-five yards up the row. There was no point in hurrying now. The tram took on its passengers, turned the corner and went on its way into Broughton. It would be half an hour before the next one followed.

Mollie went back into the house and stood quietly in the hall, wondering whether she ought not to work some more at the rug instead of going into Broughton to see the moving picture. But tomorrow was the Sabbath and this was the one night in the week she called her own; to break the routine she had made of the last four years was hard to do. It was the routine that had helped her forget how long four years could be.

She went back into the parlor and took off her hat. She looked at the rug and even picked up the hook, then she laid it down again. She touched a match to the wick in the lamp, turned it low, and then stood for some minutes considering her reflection in the mirror. She did not think she had changed much. Archie would find little difference in her if he came home now. An idea crossed her mind and she looked about the room until her eyes found a small framed photograph on the top shelf of the whatnot. She took it down and went back to the mirror, comparing her reflection with the girl in the picture until she admitted to herself that she had changed a great deal. She looked no more than a child in that wedding photograph as she stood hanging onto Archie's arm. They had both been so young; Archie twenty and she three years younger. She looked at Archie's thick hair and remembered the way it felt when her fingers brushed it the wrong way. He had never been able to part his hair, it had been so stiff. Even in that poor picture his eyes looked hurt and exposed, and no wonder, she thought, with the life his father had made for him. She had been the first person in all Broughton to understand and admire Archie —before he became a hero whom nobody understood and everyone admired.

She put the photograph back on the whatnot and then sighed without realizing she was doing so, as she passed the palms of her hands down the neat curves of her hips and flanks. For the first time in four years a thought opened wide in her mind as she tried to examine it. Would Archie ever come home? It was more than a year since he had sent any money and eight months since she had even received a postcard from him. But she knew where he was at the moment, and that was a lot more than she usually knew about him.

Did Archie ever intend to come home? She put the thought away again as she pulled open a drawer in the table by the window and took out a piece of newspaper which she had folded and stuffed in there the day before. Spreading it out flat on the table, she turned up the lamp and began to read it slowly, beginning with the Halifax dateline under the banner on the sports page. Archie's name was often to be found in this column, but never before had there been so much.

> Up from New York comes word that Archie MacNeil's next opponent is being groomed for a shot at Jack Dillon's light-heavyweight title. They say this boy Packy Miller is quite a slugger and you can get odds at four to one that he'll beat Archie, and two to one he'll win by the knockout route. The fight's to be held in Trenton, New Jersey, by the way, Miller's home town.
>
> If these odds are anywhere near right, all we can say is that Archie has gone a long way over the hill. We saw Packy Miller in Boston last fall, and the boy who fought that night couldn't have stayed in the same ring with the Archie MacNeil who flattened Tim O'Leary two years ago that great night in Providence.

Mollie remembered the fight with O'Leary, remembered what Archie's victory had meant to the men of Broughton and all the collieries roundabout. They had been as happy as though something beautiful had come into the lives of them all. She read on.

> Archie's decline from the status of top-line contender to a trial horse fighting for peanuts calls for some pretty sharp questions about how well he's been managed. A long time ago—three months after the O'Leary fight to be exact—this column noted that Archie MacNeil was battling at the rate of once every ten days. What fighter can stand a pace like that? He was sent in at catchweights against George Chip before his left eye was healed from an old cut. Chip was ten pounds lighter, but he also happened to be the middleweight champion of the world, and what he did to Archie's eye that night wasn't funny. To our way of thinking, that particular fight was the turning point in the career of the boy from the mines.
>
> Make no mistake, this boy Packy Miller is no George Chip. The odds may be heavy, but we have a hunch that Archie is going to win this one. He better had, because if he can't beat Miller there's no place else for him to go.

Mollie read the last sentence over again and tried to realize that the words referred to her husband. When she and Archie were married there had been no question of his becoming a prize fighter. That he was a brave and a good boxer she had known; so were lots of other boys in Broughton. She had even known that he was fierce, unpredicatble, hated his work in the mine and sometimes got roaring drunk. So did many others. But she had always been able to quiet him and control him until he was calm again. Alan was too little to remember the excitement when his father won the middleweight championship of Canada in a fight in Halifax, thereby astonishing and delighting the whole of Cape Breton Island. Then the fat man with the bowler hat had come up from the Boston States to offer him big money for fighting.

Mollie closed her eyes and clasped her hands as she remembered the man. He had been so dreadful and Archie had not been able to see it. He was fat and pasty and his voice was a thin falsetto. He had only half a nose, and when she asked Archie what had happened to it, Archie laughed and told her that somebody had bitten it off years ago. That was the first time she had felt a whisper of fear that she might lose Archie. His lovely body—wide in the shoulders, narrow in the waist with rippling muscles all over—this was to be turned into a punching machine by an ugly fat man whose man was Sam Downey.

But to the men of Broughton, Archie was a hero. When he gave an exhibition before going away, six thousand Highlanders — men who had been driven from the outdoors into the pits where physical courage had become almost the only virtue they could see clearly and see all the time — paid to watch him fight. They loved him because he was giving significance, even a crude beauty, to the clumsy courage they all felt in themselves.

Mollie stuffed the newspaper back in the drawer and went out to the kitchen to look at the alarm clock. The next tram was due in twelve minutes, but she wanted to get out of the house. She left the door unlocked so that Mrs. MacDonald could come in later in the evening, and began walking slowing toward the corner.

It was a far different scene now from the one which she and Alan had passed on their way home from the beach that afternoon. The miners' row was quiet. The sun had set and the long afterglow of a June evening was flooding scattered clouds with red and saffron and then with bronze. Below the clouds the earth was darkening fast and the whole area seemed uncannily silent with the men in town for Saturday night.

"And where do you think *you're* going?"

Mollie started at the bitterness in the voice and brought her eyes down from the sky to see the withered face of Mrs. MacCuish staring at her from the steps of a neighboring house. The old woman's husband had been killed in a mine accident fifteen years before, and one of her sons was married and two others had gone to the States. The old woman sat alone on her steps smoking a clay pipe and looking up and down the row. Mollie disregarded her because it was said that she was no longer right in her mind.

"All day long you do nothing at all whateffer and in the night you enjoy yourself. You whill pay for it when himself comes home."

Mollie was relieved when she had passed the old woman and was out of earshot, for the old voice was thin and high. Other women sitting on their doorsteps spoke to her in kind soft voices and she answered them. The women were always on the steps on a fine evening like this when their men were in town. They sat there in the gathering twilight whispering like spirits, some of the older ones speaking in Gaelic, the others in English with a strong Gaelic accent. As she passed the fourth house, Mollie saw that the women on the steps were turning to look further up the row where Angus the Barraman, another MacNeil though no relation of Archie, was kneeling on the ground in front of a washtub. His wife stood over him, and everyone in the row knew this meant that Angus had escaped his wife before she had been able to get her hands on his pay and had got drunk before he had even washed the coal dust off his face. As Mollie neared them she could hear Mrs. Angus scolding and Angus grunting back at her through a foam of suds.

Something she said which Mollie couldn't hear must have been more than he could take, for suddenly he rose in a rage and heaved over the tub. The water splashed her skirt and her shoes as he stood there, lean, angular, wet and only half-washed.

Out of the suds came his voice. "Hold your tongue, woman, or by Chesus, I whill be angry at you!"

"Your own wife," said Mrs. Angus, ignoring the water at her feet, "and efferybody looking at you, and efferybody able to hear you, moreoffer!"

"You and the lot of them!" The Barraman shouted. "There iss a place where you can go!"

"And what whill Father Donald be saying when I tell him

where the pay hass gone this week?"

"Father Donald hass my permission to buggerize hisself iff he would say a man cannot spend hiss pay without the old woman foreffer asking where it goes. Would I be saying no to Red Whillie when he iss happy?"

"Red Whillie! So it wass him you wass with? I might haff known it."

Angus picked up the tub in both hands and smashed it down on the ground. The wood was too well seasoned to break, but the tub bounced and hit his wife on the foot and she began to jump up and down on one leg, holding the ankle of the other.

"Into the house, by Chesus," Mollie heard Angus roar, "or I whill show you what else I can do!"

Mrs. Angus gave him a bitter look before she turned her back and limped into the house. As the door slammed behind her, Angus the Barraman sat down on his front step, the suds beginning to melt on his face and the wet coal dust like a black scum patching his naked chest and flanks. He sat there with his chin in his hands staring across the road at the field beyond, and Mollie took care not to look at him as she passed, for when the Barraman was sober he was always conscious of his dignity and she did not wish to embarrass him now by watching him when he was at a disadvantage.

When she had passed she could hear him begin to croon a Gaelic song to himself. It was as soft and plaintive as the cry of a sea bird lost in the fog.

The reason for the tart remarks Mrs. MacCuish had made became apparent as she neared the lamppost with the white band around it, at the corner. Louis Camire was standing under it, and from his position she knew he had probably been waiting for some time.

"Hullo," she said when she reached him, letting him see that she was glad to find him there.

"I thought maybe you would be going into town tonight," he said without emphasis. *"Mon Dieu,* it is a miserable place, that theatre, but it is a place to go."

She noticed that Camire was wearing his best suit, the one he had bought in Sydney which always made him look more foreign than when he was in working clothes. Compared to the bulky Highlanders of Broughton, he seemed a very small man. Even with his padded shoulders he looked frail, but she knew he was wiry and quick, for he had already earned the reputation of being able to take care of himself.

"You look verree nice," he said in his strong French accent. "Some day I would like to buy you fine clothes." He shrugged his shoulders. "But there are no fine clothes 'ere. What a place!"

"It is not so bad as you think it is," she said.

She forced herself to look away from him. For four years she had been alone except for Alan; it made her afraid of the look in his eyes. She still knew little about him. It was believed that he had run away from France to escape military service. It was an explanation which satisfied those who could think of no other reason why a young Frenchman should have been sailing under the Italian flag and then elected not to return with his mates from the wrecked ship. Whenever Mollie asked him about France his voice became wistful. His father had a business in an ancient town in the south of France, he said. Some day he might go back to it. He said he was a socialist and that a great revolution was coming. For a time he had tried to advance himself in the local of the union, but he got nowhere with the men, who were friendly enough to him personally while they dismissed him as a foreigner who talked too much. To Mollie he talked about many things she could not understand, and he wanted to talk about other things she understood only too well. That was why she was half afraid of him. She knew he wanted to be her lover and she knew he was even more lonely than she was herself. On an evening like this she tried not to think about the feeling he gave her.

"'Ow is the boy?" he asked.

"Oh, we had such a lovely afternoon on the shore! He is asleep now. At least I hope he is." Her expression changed. "Louis, something is the matter with your eyes! They're all red."

He shrugged. "Coal smoke is not an ointment for ophthalmia."

"You ought to see Dr. Ainslie."

"I would have to be very sick before I see 'im."

"But Dr. Ainslie would help you. He is the best doctor in the whole town."

"Me, I think 'e is a son of a bitch."

"If you would know him," Mollie went on eagerly, "you would not think so. He is the kindest man. Alan goes to play by the brook near his house and the doctor lets him. Whenever Mrs. Ainslie sees him she always speaks to him." As Camire made no comment she added, "Mrs. Ainslie is very fond of children, I shouldn't wonder."

Camire rolled a cigarette, twisted the end, lifted his foot and scratched a match on the sole of his pointed tan shoe. He spoke through a puff of tobacco smoke, his eyes squinting as some of the smoke got into them and irritated their already smarting membranes.

"This wife of the *docteur*," he said, "she is another thing. She 'as a figure like a statue before the Hotel de Ville in my town." He made generous curving movements with his hands. "But what does she do with a figure like that, eh? Not one damn thing. No children. Name of God! Or maybe it is the *docteur* that is no good."

Mollie broke into a soft musical laugh. She knew it was only his way, to talk like this.

"There is nothing the matter with Mrs. Ainslie," she said. "Or with the doctor, either. Everybody knows they have had bad luck."

He pointed his cigarette at her. "According to you, there is nothing the matter with anybody. You like them all. When some woman 'as a baby, you go in to wash her dishes for her." The cigarette kept jerking towards her to emphasize his points. "That *docteur!* Sometimes 'e says good-morning. So that makes 'im a lovely man." Again the cigarette jerked. "That is why you are always the underdog."

She wanted Camire to be happy, and she wanted him to like her and to understand that people here were kind no matter what people were like in France.

"No, Louis — the doctor is a special man. He knows more than we do and he works so hard he sometimes goes two or three whole days without even sleeping."

Camire shrugged his shoulders. She could not understand why he made things so hard for himself and it troubled her.

"This *docteur*," He said, "'e talks to people like dirt."

"He's just tired, and everybody knows he has no patience with nonsense."

"'E thinks 'e is better than everybody else. Does 'e say *Mister* Camire? Does 'e say *Mister* MacDonald? No. But who pays 'im? The workers pay 'im. Every month thirty cents comes off their pay for that fine 'ouse 'e lives in. You are the bosses, but every time 'e comes along, what 'appens? You take off your caps and thank 'im for doing what you pay 'im for." Camire kicked a pebble with his pointed shoe. "Let me tell you something. There is no future in being the underdog."

She put her hand on his arm to quiet his excitement. "But, Louis, nobody here is an underdog."

"No?" He looked at her with a scorn she knew was not for herself but for the ideas she held. He pointed to the hideous mass of the bankhead towering up to the sky on his right. "Who owns that?"

"The company owns it, of course."

"And 'ow much money would the company make if you did not let yourselves be underdogs? This is Saturday night. At MacDonald's Corner there will soon be at least fifty men fighting each other. Do they fight the company? No, they fight with their fists against each other, every Saturday night, for the sport."

"But nobody wants another strike. Four years ago there was a terrible strike. And the men like fighting. It makes them feel better to show each other what they can do."

His short silence made her hope that he might be trying to understand her point, but when he spoke again she sighed.

"You admire this *docteur,*" he said, "because you think the education is a fine thing, and 'e 'as maybe just a little bit of education. At the same time you admire that *salaud* Red Willie MacIsaac because *le bon Dieu* gave 'im a body ten times too big for the brain of the mouse that 'e 'as in 'is 'ead. You —"

"But nobody admires Red Willie!" She was laughing at him.

"So you stay the underdogs. Because you think it is better to be Scottish than to 'ave some sense. You think it is better to 'ave the big fist than to 'ave the big brain."

She pressed his arm with her fingers. "Louis, you don't understand. Everybody admires Dr. Ainslie because he has a very big brain. The men know he likes them even when he scolds them. They know he wants them to improve."

He looked at her with exasperation. Then his eyes softened and he drew closer to her, folded her hand under his arm and stopped talking. They stood quietly for several minutes waiting for the tram, but the long slope down to the bridge remained empty and there was no sound of wheels grinding in the distance.

"When I made shipwreck," he said more quietly, "I said to myself, so — this is a new country and I am sick of waiting for the revolution to change things at 'ome. I will stay 'ere. So I stay, and what the 'ell do I find? I find it is older than France. There is no organization. Labour in France — that is something. It 'as organization. But 'ere you do not even know the most necessary thing. The men who run the world, they are sons of bitches, and you do not know that." Then he smiled at her and his eyes were liquid. "But you are 'ere, too, and you are something else. Me, I am the one man in this place that knows what you could be."

She knew it was better to smile than to say anything. The loneliness in his eyes was so great she wanted to stroke his forehead to take the look away.

Alistair MacLeod / Inverness

Alistair MacLeod was born in Alberta in 1936 but grew up in Inverness County, the birthplace of his parents. He attended the Nova Scotia Teachers' College, St. Francis Xavier University, the University of New Brunswick and the University of Notre Dame. He has worked as a milkman, logger, miner and public relations man but since 1969 has taught English and Creative Writing at the University of Windsor where he is also fiction editor of **The University of Windsor Review.**

The Lost Salt Gift of Blood, a collection of short stories was published in 1976. "The Tuning of Perfection" is a new story and appears in print here for the first time.

The Tuning of Perfection

by Alistair MacLeod

    He thought of himself, in the middle of that April, as a man who had made it through another winter. He was seventy-eight years old and it seems best to give his exact age now, rather than trying to rely on such descritpions as "old" or "vigorous" or "younger than his years." He was seventy-eight and a tall, slim man with dark hair and brown eyes and his own teeth. He was frequently described as "neat" because he always appeared clean-shaven and the clothes he wore were always clean and in order. He wore suspenders instead of a belt, because he felt they kept his trousers "inline" instead of allowing them to sag sloppily down his waist, revealing too much of his shirt. And when he went out in public, he always wore shoes. In cold or muddy weather, he wore overshoes or rubbers or what he called "overboots" — the rubber kind with the zippers in the front, to protect his shoes. He never wore the more common rubber boots in public — although, of course, he owned them and kept them neatly on a piece of clean cardboard in a corner of his porch.
    He lived alone near the top of the mountain in a house which he himself had built when he was a much younger man. There had once been another house in the same clearing, and the hollow of its cellar was still visible as well as a few of the moss covered stones which had formed its early foundation. This "ex-house" had been built by his great grandfather, shortly after he had come from the Isle of Skye and it was still referred to as "the firsthouse" or sometimes as "the old house" although it was no longer there. No one was really sure why his great grandfather had built the house so high up on the mountain, especially when one considered that he had been granted a great deal of land and there

were more accessible spots upon it where one might build a house. Some thought that since he was a lumberman, he had wanted to start on top of the mountain and log his way down. Others thought that because of the violence he had left in Scotland, he wanted to be inaccessible in the new world, and wanted to be able to see any potential enemies before they could see him. Others thought that he had merely wanted to be alone, while another group maintained that he had built it for the view. All of the projected reasons became confused and intermingled with the passing of the generations and the distancing of the man from Skye. Perhaps the theory of the view proved the most enduring, because, although the man from Skye and the house he built were no longer visible, the view still was. And it was truly spectacular. One could see for miles along the floor of the valley and over the tops of the smaller mountains and when one looked to the west there was the sea. There, it was possible to see the various fishing boats of summer and the sealing ships of winter and the lines of Prince Edward Island and the flat shapes of the Quebec owned Magdalen Islands and, more to the east, the purple mass of Newfoundland.

The paved road or the "main road" which ran along the valley floor was five miles by automobile from his house, although it was not really that far if one walked and took various short cuts: paths and footbridges over the various tumbling brooks and creeks that spilled down the mountain's side. Once there had been a great deal of traffic on such paths; people on foot and people with horses, but over the years as more and more people obtained automobiles, the paths fell into disuse and became overgrown, and the bridges which were washed away by the spring freshets were no longer replaced very regularly nor very well.

The section of winding road that led to his house and ended in his yard had been a bone of contention for many years as had some of the other sections as well. Most of the people on the upper reaches of the mountain were his relatives and they were all on sections of the land granted to the man from Skye. Some of the road was "public" and therefore eligible to be maintained by the Department of Highways. Other sections of it, including his, were "private" so they were not maintained at all by government but only by the people living along them. As he lived a mile above the "second last" or the "second" house — depending upon which way you were counting — he did not receive visits from the grader nor the gravel truck, nor, in winter, the snowplough. It was generally assumed that the Department of Highways was secretly glad that it did not have to send its men nor its equipment up the twisting switchbacks and around the hairpin turns which skirted the treacherous gullies containing the wrecks of rolled and abandoned cars. The Department of Highways was not that fussy about the slightly lower reaches of the road either and there were always various petitions being circulated, demanding "better service for the tax dollar." Still, whenever the issue of making a "private" section of the road "public" was raised, there were always counter petitions that circulated and used phrases like "keeping the land of our fathers *ours*." Three miles down the mountain, though, (or two miles up) there was a nice wide "turn around" for the school bus, and up to and including that spot, the road was maintained as well as any other of its kind.

He did not mind living alone up on the mountain, saying that he got great television reception which was, of course, true — although it was a relatively new justification. There was no television when he built the house in the two years prior to 1927 and when he was filled with the fever of his approaching marriage. Even then, people wondered why he was "going up the mountain" while many of the others were coming down — but he paid them little mind; working at it in determined perfection in the company of his twin brother, and getting the others only when it was absolutely necessary: for the raising of the roof beams and the fitting of the gables.

He and his wife had been the same age and had been almost consumed by one another while they were still quite young. Neither had ever had another boyfriend nor girlfriend but he had told her they would not marry until he had completed the house. He wanted the house so that they could be "alone together," as soon as they were married, rather than moving in with in-laws or relatives for a while as was frequently the custom of the time. So he had worked at it determinedly and desperately, eagerly anticipating the time when he could end "his life" and begin "their lives."

He and his twin brother had built it in "the old way," which meant making their own plans and cutting all the logs themselves and "snigging" them out with their horses and setting up their own saw mill and planing mill. And deciding, also, to use wooden pegs in the roof timbers instead of nails; so that the house would move in the mountain's winds — like a ship — move but not capsize, move yet still return.

In the summer before the marriage, his wife-to-be had worked as hard as he, carrying lumber and swinging a hammer; and when her father suggested she was doing too much masculine work, she had replied, "I am doing what I want to do. I am doing it for *us.*"

During the building of their house, they often sang together and the language of their singing was Gaelic. Sometimes one of them would sing the verses and the other the chorus and, at other times, they would sing the verses and choruses together and all the way through. Some of the songs contained at least fifteen or twenty verses and it would take a long time to complete them. On clear still days all of the people living down along the mountain's side and even below in the valley could hear the banging of their hammers and the youthful power of their voices.

They were married on a Saturday in late September and their first daughter was born exactly nine months later which was an item of brief and passing interest. And their second daughter was born barely eleven months after their first. During the winter months of that time he worked in a lumber camp, some fifteen miles away. Cutting pulp for $1.75 a cord and getting $40.00 a month for his team of horses as well. Rising at 5:30 and working until after seven in the evening and sleeping on a bunk with a mattress made from boughs.

Sometimes he would come home on the weekends and on the clear, winter nights she would hear the distinctive sound of his horse's bells as they left the valley floor to begin their ascent up the mountain's side. Although the climb was steep, the horses would walk faster because they knew they were coming home, even breaking into a trot on the more level areas and causing their bells to accelerate accordingly. Sometimes he would get out of the wood sleigh and run beside the horses or ahead of them in order to keep warm and also to convince himself that he was getting home faster.

When she heard the bells, she would take the lamp and move it from one window to the other and then take it back again and continue to repeat the procedure. The effect was almost that of a regularly flashing light, like that of a light house or of someone flicking a light switch off and on at regulated intervals. He would see the light now at one window and then in the other; sent down like the regulated flashing signals his mares gave off when in heat, and, although he would be near exhausted, he would be filled with desire and urge himself upward at an even greater rate.

After he had stabled his horses and fed them, he would go into their house and they would meet one another in the middle of the kitchen floor; holding one another and going into one another, sometimes, while the snow and frost still hung so heavily on his clothes that they creaked when he moved or steamed near the presence of the stove. The lamp would be stilled on the kitchen table and they would be alone. Only the monogamous eagles who nested in the hemlock tree, even father up the mountain, seemed above them.

They were married for five years in an intensity which it seemed could never last. Going more and more into each other and excluding most others for the company of themselves.

When she went into premature labour in February of 1931, he was not at home, because it was still six weeks before the expected birth and they had decided that he would stay in the camp a little longer in order to earn the extra money they needed for their anticipated fourth child.

There had been heavy snows in the area and then high winds and then it had turned bitterly cold — all in the time span of a day and a half. It had been impossible to get down from the mountain and then almost impossible to get word to him in the camp, although his twin brother managed to walk in on the second day bringing him the news that everyone on the mountain already knew — that he had lost his wife and what might have been his first-born son. The snow was higher than his twin brother's head when they saw him coming into the camp; and he was soaked with perspiration from fighting the drifts and pale and shaking and he began to throw up in the yard of the camp almost before he could deliver his message.

He had left immediately to walk out, leaving his brother behind to rest, while following his incoming tracks back out. He could not believe it; could not believe that she had somehow gone without him,   could not believe that in their closeness he was still the last to know; and that in spite of hoping "to live alone together," she had somehow died, surrounded by others, but without him and really alone in the ultimate sense. He could not believe that in the closeness of their beginning there had been separation in their end. He had tried to hope that there might be some mistake but the image of his brother, pale and shaken and vomiting in the packed down snow of the lumber camp's yard, dispelled any such possibility.

He was numb throughout all of the funeral preparations and the funeral itself; his wife's sisters looked after his three small daughters who, while they sometimes called for their mother, seemed almost to welcome the lavish attention visited upon them. On the afternoon following the funeral, the pneumonia which his twin brother had developed after his walk into the camp, worsened and he had gone to sit beside his bed, holding his hand, at least able to be *present* this time, yet aware of the disapproving looks of Cora, his brother's wife, who was a woman he had never liked. Looks which said: "If he had not gone for *you*, this would never have happened." Sitting there while his brother's chest deepened, in spite of the poultices and the linaments and even the administrations of the doctor, who finally made it up the mountain road, and pronounced the pneumonia as "surprisingly advanced."

After the death of his brother, the numbness continued. He felt as those who lose all of their family in the midnight fire or on the sinking ship. Suddenly and without survivors. He felt guilt for his wife and for his brother's fatherless children, and for his daughters who would now never know their mother. And he felt terribly alone.

His daughters stayed with him for a while as he tried to do what their mother had done. But gradually his wife's sisters began to suggest that the girls would be better off with them. At first he opposed the idea because both he and his wife had never been overly fond of her sisters, considering them, somehow, more vulgar than they were themselves. But gradually it became apparent that if he were ever to return to the woods and earn a living, someone would have to look after three children under the age of four. He was torn for the remainder of the winter months and into spring. Sometimes appreciating what he felt was the intended kindness of his in-laws and at other times angry at certain overheard remarks: "It is not right for three little girls to be alone up on that mountain with that man, a *young* man." As if he were, somehow, more interesting as a potential child molester rather than simply as a father. Gradually his daughters began to spend evenings and weekends with their aunts and then weeks and then in the manner of small children, they no longer cried when he left nor clung to his legs, nor sat in the window to await his approach. And then they began to call him "Archibald" as did the other members of the households in which they lived; so that in the end, he seemed neither husband nor brother nor even father but only "Archibald." He was twenty-seven years old.

He had always been called Archibald or sometimes in Gaelic, "Gilleasbuig." Perhaps, because of what was perceived as a kind of formality that hung about him, no one ever called him "Arch" nor the more familiar and common "Archie." He did not look nor act "like an Archie," as they said. And with the passing of the years, letters came that were addressed simply to "Archibald" and which bore a variety of addresses covering a radius of some forty miles. Many of the letters, in the later years, came from the folklorists who had "discovered" him in the 1960's and for whom he had made various tapes and recordings. And he had come to be regarded as "the last of the authentic old time Gaelic singers." He was faithfully recorded in the archives at Sydney and in Halifax and in Ottawa and his picture had appeared in various scholarly and less scholarly journals; sometimes with the arms of the folklorists around him, sometimes holding one of his horses and sometimes standing beside his shining pickup truck which bore a bumper sticker which read "Suas Leis A' Ghaidlig." Sometimes the articles bore titles such as "Cape Breton singer: The Last of His kind" or "Holding Fast On Top of the Mountain" or "Mnemonic Devices in the Gaelic Line" — the latter generally being accompanied by a plethora of footnotes.

He did not really mind the folklorists; enunciating the words over and over again for them, explaining that "bh" was pronounced as "v" (like the "ph" in phone is pronounced "f" he would say), expanding on the more archaic meanings and footnoting, himself, the words and phrases of local origin. Doing it all with care and seriousness in much the same way that he filed and set his saws or structured his woodpile.

Now, in this April of the 1980's he thought of himself, as I said earlier, as a man of seventy-eight years who had made it through another winter. He had come to terms with most things, although never really with the death of his wife; but that too had become easier during the last decades, although he was still bothered by the sexual references which came because of his monastic existence.

Scarcely a year after "the week of deaths," he had been visited by Cora, his twin brother's wife. She had come with her breath reeking of rum and placed the bottle on the middle of his kitchen table.

"I've been thinking," she said. "It's time me and you got together."

"Mmmm," he said, trying to make the most non-commital sound he could think of.

"Here," she said, going to his cupboard and taking down two of his sparkling glasses and splashing rum into them . "Here," she said, sliding a glass toward him across the table and seating herself opposite him. "Here, have a shot of this. It will put lead in your pencil," and then after a pause, "although from what I've *heard* there's no need of that."

He was taken aback. Somehow imagining her and his twin brother lying side by side at night discussing his physicality. "Heard *what?*" he wondered, *"Where?"*

"Yeah," she said. "There's not much need of you being up here on this mountain by yourself and me being by myself farther down. If you don't use it, it'll rust off."

He was close to panic, finding her so lonely and so drunkenly available and so much unlike the memory of his own wife. He wondered if she remembered how much they disliked each other— or thought they did. And he wondered if he were somehow thought of as being interchangeable with his dead brother. As if, because they were twins, their bodies must somehow be the same, regardless of their minds.

"I bet it's rusty right now," she said and she leaned the upper part of her body across the table so that he could smell the rum heavy on her breath even as he felt her fingers on his leg.

"Mmmm," he said, getting up rapidly and walking towards the window. He was rattled by her overt sexuality, the way a shy middle-aged married man might be when taken on a visit to a brothel far from his home — not because what is discussed is so foreign to him, but rather because of the manner and the approach.

Outside the window, the eagles were flying up the mountain; carrying the twigs, some of them almost branches, for the building of their home.

"Mmmm," he said, still looking out the window and down the winding road to the valley floor below.

"Well," she said, getting up and downing her drink. "I guess there's no fun here. I just wanted to say hello."

"Yes," he said. "Well, thank-you."

She lurched toward the door and he wondered if he should open it for her or if that would be too rash.

But she opened it herself.

"Well," she said as she went out into the yard. "You know where I'm at."

"Yes," he said, gaining confidence from her departing back, "I know where you are."

Now on this morning in April, half a century later, he looked out his window at the eagles flying by. They were going down into the valley to hunt, leaving their nest with their four precious eggs for the briefest time. Then he recognized the sound of the truck's motor. He recognized it before it entered the yard, in the way his wife had once recognized the individual sound of his horse's bells. The truck was muddy and splattered; not merely from this spring trip up the mountain but from a sort of residual dirt, perhaps from the previous fall. It belonged to his married granddaughter who had been christened Sarah, but preferred to be known as Sal. She wheeled her truck into the yard, getting out of it inches from his door and almost before it had stopped. She wore her hair in a ponytail although she seemed, perhaps, too old for that and her tight fitting jeans were slipped inside her husband's rubber boots. He was always slightly surprised at her ability to chew gum and smoke cigarettes at the same time and was reminded of that now as she came through his door, her lipstick leaving a red ring around her cigarette as she removed it from her mouth and flicked it out into the yard. She wore a tight-fitting T-shirt with the words, "I'm Busted" across her chest.

"Hi Archibald," she said, sitting in the chair nearest the window.

"Hi," he said.

"What's new?" she asked.

"Oh, nothing much," he replied, and then after a pause, "Would you like some tea?"

"Okay," she said. "No milk. I'm watching my figure."

"Mmmm," he said.

He looked at her from the distance of his years, trying to find within her some flashes of his wife or even of himself. She was attractive in her way, with her dark eyes and ready mouth, although shorter than either he or his wife had been at a similar age.

"Had two phone calls," she said.

"Oh," he said, always feeling a bit guilty that he had no telephone and that messages had to be left with others farther down the mountain.

"One is from a guy who wants to buy your mare. You're still interested in selling?"

"Yes, I guess so."

"The other is about Gaelic singing. They want us to sing in Halifax this summer. This is the year of "Scots Around the World." All kinds of people will be there — even some of the Royal Family. We'll be there for a week. They haven't decided on the pay yet but it'll be okay and they'll pay our accommodation and our transportation."

"Oh," he said, becoming interested and cautious at the same time. "What do you mean by us?"

"*Us.* You know, the family. They want twenty of us. There'll be a few days of rehearsal there and then some concerts and we'll be on television. I can hardly wait. I have to do lots of shopping in Halifax and it will be a chance to sleep in without Tom bothering me. We won't even have to be at the theatre or studio or whatever until noon." She lit another cigarette.

"What do they want us to sing?" he asked.

"Oh, who cares?" she said. "It's the trip that's important. Some of the old songs. They're coming to audition us or something in two or three weeks. We'll sing *"Fear A'Bhata"* or something," she said and butting her cigarette on her saucer and laying her gum beside it on the table, she began to sing in a clear powerful voice:

>*Fhir a' bhata, no ho ro eile,*
>*Fhir a' bhata, na ho ro eile,*

Fhir a' bhata, na ho ro eile,
Mho shoraidh slan leat 's gach ait' an teid thu

Is tric me 'sealltainn o'n chnoc a's airde
Dh'fheuch am faic mi fear a' bhata,
An tig thu 'n diugh, no 'n tig thu 'maireach;
'S mur tig thu idir, gur truagh a ta mi.

Only when she sang did she remind him, somewhat, of his wife and again he felt the hope that she might somehow reach that standard of excellence.

"You're singing it too fast," he said cautiously when she had finished. "But it is good. You're singing it like a milling song. It's supposed to be a lament — for a loved one that's lost."

He sang it himself, slowly, and stressing the distinction of each syllable.

She seemed interested for a while, listening intently before replacing her gum and lighting another cigarette, then tossing the still lighted match into the stove.

"Do you know what the words mean?" he said, when he had finished.

"No," she said. "Neither will anybody else. I just make the noises. I've been hearing the things since I was two. I know how they go. I'm not dumb you know."

"Who else are they asking?" he said, partially out of interest and partially to change the subject and to avoid confrontation.

"I don't know," she said. "They said they'd get back to us later. All they wanted to know now was if we were interested. The man about the mare will be up later. I got to go now."

She was out of the door almost immediately, turning her truck in a spray of gravel that flicked against his house, the small stones pinging against his window pane. A muddied bumper sticker read: "If you're horny, honk your horn."

He was reminded, as he often was, of Cora who had been dead now for some fifteen years, and who had married another man within a year of her visit to him with her open proposal. And he was touched that this granddaughter should seem so much like his brother's wife instead of like his own.

The man who came to buy the mare was totally unlike any other horse buyer he had ever seen. He came in a suit and in an elaborate car and spoke in an accent that was difficult to identify. He was accompanied by Carver , who was apparently his guide and who was a violent young man in his thirties from the other side of the mountain. Carver's not un-handsome face was marred by a series of raised grey scars and his upper lip had been thickened as a result of a fight in which someone had swung a logging chain into his mouth; an action which had also cost him the loss of his most obvious teeth. He wore his wallet on a chain hooked to his belt and scuffed his heavy lumberman's boots on the cardboard in Archibald's porch before entering the kitchen. He sat by the window and rolled a cigarette while the horse buyer talked to Archibald.

"How old is the mare?"

"Five," said Archibald.

"Has she ever had a colt?"

"Why yes," said Archibald, puzzled by the question. Usually buyers asked if the horse would work single or double or something about its disposition, or its legs or its chest. Or if it would work in snow, or if it would eat enough to sustain a heavy work schedule.

"Do you think she could have another colt?" he asked.

"Why, I suppose," he said, almost annoyed, "if she had a stallion."

"No problem," said the man.

"But," said Archibald, driven by his old honesty, "she has never worked. I have not been in the woods that much lately and I always used the old mare, her mother, before she died. I planned to train her but never got around to it. She's more like a pet. She probably will work though. They've always worked. It's in the stock. I've had them all my life." He stopped almost embarrassed at having to apologize for his horses and for himself.

"Okay," said the man. "No problem. She has had a colt though?"

"Look," said Carver from his seat near the window, and snuffing out his cigarette between his calloused thumb and forefinger, "he already told you that. I told you this man don't lie."

"Okay," said the man, taking out his cheque book.

"Don't you want to see her first?" asked Archibald.

"No, it's okay," the man said. "I believe you."

"He wants $900.00," said Carver. "She's a young mare."

"Okay," said the man to Archibald's amazement. He himself, having been hopeful of perhaps $700.00 or even less, since she had never worked.

"You'll take her down in your truck later?" the man said to Carver.

"Right on!" said Carver, and they left together. The man driving with a peculiar caution as if he had never been off pavement before and was afraid that the woods might swallow him.

After they left, Archibald went out to his barn to talk to the mare. He led her out to the brook to drink and led her to the door of the house where she waited while he went in and rummaged for some bread to offer her as a farewell treat. She was young and strong and splendid and he was somehow disappointed that the buyer had not, at least, seen her so that he could appreciate her excellent qualities.

Shortly after noon Carver drove his truck into the yard. "Do you want a beer?" he said to Archibald, motioning toward the open case on the seat beside him."

"No, I don't think so," Archibald said. "We may as well get this over with."

"Okay," said Carver. "Do you want to lead her on?"

"No, it's okay," said Archibald. "She'll go with anybody."

"Yeah," said Carver, "Perhaps that's a good way to be."

They went into the barn. In spite of what he had said, Archibald found himself going up beside the mare and untying the rope and leading her out into the afternoon sun which reflected on her dappled shining coat. Carver backed his truck up to a small incline beside the barn and lowered the tailgate. Then Archibald handed him the rope and watched as she followed him willingly into the truck.

"This is the last of all them nice horses you had up here, eh?" said Carver after he had tied the rope and swung down from the truck.

"Yes," said Archibald, "the last."

"I guess you hauled a lot of wood with them horses. I heard guys talking, older guys, who worked with you in the camps."

"Oh, yes," said Archibald.

"I heard guys say you and your brother could cut seven cords of pulp a day with a cross cut saw, haul it and stack it."

"Oh yes," he said. "Some days we could. Days seemed longer

then," he added with a smile.

"Christ we're lucky to get seven with a power saw unless we're in a real good stand," said Carver pulling up his trousers and starting to roll a cigarette. "Your timber here on your own land is as good as ever they say."

"Yes," he said. "It's pretty good."

"That Archibald, they say, no one knows where he gets all them logs, hauls them out with them horses and doesn't seem to disturb anything. Year after year. Treats the mountain as if it were a garden."

"Mmmm," he said.

"Not like now, eh? We just cut 'em all down. Go in with heavy equipment, tree farmers and loaders and do it all in a day, to hell with tomorrow."

"Yes," said Archibald. "I've noticed."

"You don't want to sell?" asked Carver.

"No," he said. "Not yet."

"I just thought, . . . since you were letting your mare go. No work for the mare, no work for you."

"Oh, she'll probably work somewhere," he said. "I'm not so sure about myself."

"Nah, she won't work," said Carver. "They want her for birth control pills."

"For what?" said Archibald.

"This guy says, I don't know if it's true, that there's this farm outside of Montreal that's connected to a lab or something. Anyway they've got all these mares there and they keep them bred all the time and they use their water for birth control pills."

It seemed so preposterous that Archibald was not sure how to react. He scrutinized Carver's scarred yet open face, looking for a hint, some kind of touch but he could find nothing.

"Yeah," said Carver. "They keep the mares pregnant all the time so the women won't be."

"What do they do with the colts?" said Archibald, thinking that he might try a question for a change.

"I dunno," said Carver. "He didn't say. I guess they just throw them away."

"Got to go now," he said swinging into the cab of his truck, "and take her down the mountain. I think he's almost got a box car of these mares, or a transport truck. In two days she'll be outside Montreal and they'll get her a stallion and that'll be it."

The truck roared into action and moved from the incline near the barn. Archibald had been closer to it than he thought and was forced to step out of the way. As it passed, Carver rolled down the window and shouted, "Hey, Archibald, do you sing anymore?"

"Not so much," he said.

"Got to talk to you about that, sometime," he said, above the engine's roar and then he and the truck and the splendid mare left the yard to begin their switchbacked journey down the mountain.

For a long time Archibald did not know what to do. He felt somehow betrayed by forces he could not control. The image of his mare beneath the weight of successive and different stallions came to his mind but the most haunting image was that of the dead colts which Carver had described as being "thrown away." He imagined them, somehow, as the many dead unwanted animals he had seen; thrown out on the manure piles behind the barns, perhaps with their skulls smashed in by blows from axes. He doubted that there was anything quite like that outside of Montreal and he doubted — or wanted to doubt — somehow more than he could, what Carver had said. But he had no way to verify the facts nor to disprove them and the images persisted. He thought, as he always did at times of loss, of his wife. And then of the pale, still body of his quiet and unbreathing son; with the intricate blue veins winding like the maplines of roads and rivers upon his fragile, delicate skull. Both wife and son gone from him — taken it always seemed in the winter's snow. And he felt, somehow, that he might cry.

He looked up to the sound of the whooshing eagles' wings. They were flying up the mountain, almost wavering in their flight. Like weary commuters trying to make it home. He had watched them through the long winter as they were forced to fly farther and farther in search of food and open water. He had noticed the dullness of their feathers and the dimming lustre in their intense green eyes. Now, and he was not sure, if perhaps it was his eyesight or his angle of vision, the female's wing tips seemed almost to graze the still bare branches of the reaching trees and it seemed like she might falter and fall. And then, the male who had gone on ahead, turned and came back, gliding on the wind with his wings outstretched, trying to conserve what little energy, he, himself,

107

had left. He passed so close to Archibald that he could see, or imagined that he could see, the desperate fear in his fierce, defiant eyes. He was so intent on his mission that he paid little attention to Archibald, circling beside his mate until their wing tips almost touched. She seemed to gain strength from his presence and almost to lunge with her wings, like a desperate swimmer on her final lap and they continued, together, up the mountain. In the dampness of the late Spring, Archibald feared, as perhaps did they, for the future of their four potential young.

He had seen the eagles in other seasons and circumstances. He had seen the male seize a branch in his powerful talons and soar toward the sky in the sheer exhuberance of his power and strength; had seen him snap the branch in two (in the way a strong man might snap a kindling across his knee) letting the two sections fall towards the earth before plummeting after one or the other and snatching it from the air; wheeling and somersaulting and flipping the branch in front of him and swooping under it again and again until, tired of the game, he let it fall disinterestedly to earth.

And he had seen them in the aerial courtship of their mating; had seen them feinting and swerving high above the mountain, outlined against the sky. Had seen them come together, and with talons locked, fall cartwheeling over and over for what seemed like hundreds of feet down towards the land. Separating and braking, like lucky parachutists, at the last minute and gliding individually and parallel to the earth before starting their ascent once more.

The folklorists were always impressed by the bald eagles.

"How long have they been here?" the first group asked.

"Forever, I guess," had been his answer.

And after doing research, they had returned and said. "Yes, Cape Breton is the largest nesting area on the eastern seaboard north of Florida. And the largest east of the Rockies. It's funny, hardly anybody knows they're here."

"Oh, some people do," Archibald said with a smile.

"It's only because they don't use pesticides or hericides in the forest industry," the folklorists said. "If they start, the eagles will be gone. There are hardly any nests anymore in New Brunswick or in Maine."

"Mmmm," he said.

In the days that followed they tried to prepare for the "singing," in Halifax. They had several practices — most of them at Sal's because she had talked to the producer and had become the contact person, and also because she seemed to want to go the most. They managed to gather a number of people of varying talent — some more reluctant than others. One or two of the practices were held at Archibald's. The number in the group varied. It expanded, sometimes, to as many as thirty, including various in-laws and friends of in-laws and sometimes, people who simply had little else to do on a given evening. Throughout it all, Archibald tried to maintain control and to do it in "his way" which meant enunciating the words clearly and singing the exact number of verses in the proper order. Sometimes the attention of the younger people wandered, and sometimes the evenings deteriorated quite early and quite rapidly, with people drifting off into little knots to gossip or to tell jokes or to drink, what was in Archibald's opinion, too much. As the pressures of the spring season increased and many of the men left logging to fish or to work upon their land, there were fewer and fewer male voices at the practice sessions. Sometimes the men joked about this and the future make-up of the group.

"Do you think you'll be able to handle all these women by yourself in Halifax, Archibald?" someone might ask, although not really asking the question of him.

"Sure, he will," another voice would respond. "He's well rested. He hasn't used it in fifty years — not that we know of anyway."

Then at one practice, Sal announced with some agitation that she had been talking to the producer in Halifax. He had told her, she said, that two other groups from the area had contacted him and that he would be auditioning them as well. He would be coming in about ten days.

Everyone was dumbfounded.

"What other groups?" asked Archibald.

"One," said Sal, pausing for dramatic effect, "is headed by *Carver.*"

"Carver!" they said in unison and disbelief. And then in the midst of laud guffaws, "Carver can't sing. He can hardly speak any Gaelic. Where will he get a group?"

"Don't ask me," said Sal, "unless it's those guys he hangs

around with."

"Who else?" said Archibald.

"MacKenzies!" she said.

No one laughed at the mention of MacKenzies. They had been, traditionally, one of the oldest and best of the singing families. They lived some twenty miles away in a small and isolated valley, but Archibald had noticed over the past fifteen years or so, more and more of their houses becoming shuttered and boarded, and a few of the older ones starting to lean and even to fall to the pressures of the wind.

"They don't have enough people anymore," someone said.

"No," added another voice. "All of their best singers have gone to Toronto."

"There are two very good young men there," said Archibald, remembering a concert of a few years back, when he had seen the two, standing straight and tall a few feet back from the microphone, had seen them singing clearly and effortlessly with never a waver, nor a mispronunciation nor a missed note.

"They've gone to Calgary," said a third voice. "They've been there, now, for over a year."

"I was talking to some people from over that way, after the call from Halifax," said Sal. "They said that the MacKenzie's grandmother was going to ask them to come back. They said she was going to try to get all her singers to come home."

Archibald was touched in spite of himself. Touched that Mrs. MacKenzie would try so hard. He looked around the room and realized that there were very few people in it who realized that Mrs. MacKenzie was his cousin and, also, by extension theirs. Although he did not know her well, and had only nodded to her and exchanged a few words with her over a lifetime, he felt very close to her now. He was not even sure of the degree of the relationship (although he would work it out later) remembering now, only the story of the young woman from an earlier generation of his family who had married the young man from the valley of the MacKenzies who was of the "wrong religion." There had been great bitterness at the time and the families had refused to speak to one another til all of those who knew what the "right religion" was had died. The young woman who left had never visited her parents nor they her. It seemed sad now to Archibald, feeling almost more kinship to the scarcely known Mrs.

MacKenzie than to those members of his own direct flesh and blood who seemed now so agitated and so squabbly.

"She will never get them home," said the last voice. "They've all got jobs and responsibilities. They can't drop everything and come here or to Halifax for a week to sing four or five songs."

The voice proved right, although in the following ten days before the producer's visit, Archibald thought often of Mrs. MacKenzie making her phone calls, and of her messengers fanned out across Toronto, visiting the suburbs and the taverns, asking the question to which they already knew the answer, but feeling obliged to ask it nonetheless. In the end four MacKenzies came home, two young men who had been hurt at work and were on compensation and a middle-aged daughter and her husband who managed to take a week of their vacation earlier than usual. The *really* good young men were unable to come.

When the producer came, he brought with him two assistants with clipboards. They were all men. The producer himself was an agitated young man in his early thirties. He had curly dark hair, and wore thick glasses and a maroon t-shirt with "If you've got it, flaunt it," emblazoned across the front. When he spoke, he nervously twisted his right ear lobe.

Archibald's group was the last of the three he visited. "He's saved the best for the last," laughed Sal, not very convincingly.

He came in the evening and explained the situation briefly. If chosen, they would be in Halifax for six days. They would practice and acquaint themselves with the surroundings for the first two days and on the next four there would be a concert each evening. There would be various acts from throughout the province. They would be on television and radio both and some of the Royal Family would be in attendance.

Then he said, "Look, I really don't understand your language so we're here mainly to look for effect. We'd like you to be ready with three songs. And then maybe we'll have to cut it back to two. We'll see how it goes."

They began to sing, sitting around the table as if they were "waulking the cloth", as their ancestors had done before them. Archibald sat at the head of the table, singing loudly and clearly while the other voices rose to meet him. The producer and his assistants took notes.

"Okay, that's enough," he said after about an hour and a half.

"We'll take the third one," he said to one of his assistants.

"What's it called?" he said to Archibald.

"Mo Chridhe Trom ," said Archibald. It means "My Heart is Heavy."

"Okay," said the producer. "Let's do it again."

They began. By the twelfth verse the music took hold of Archibald in a way that he had almost forgotten it could. His voice rose and soared above the other with such clear and precise power that they faltered and were stilled.

> *'S ann air cul nam beanntan ard,*
> *Tha aite comhnuidh mo ghraidh,*
> *Fear dha 'm bheil an cridhe blath,*
> *Do'n tug mi 'n gradh a leon mi.*

> *'S ann air cul a' bhalla chloich,*
> *'S math an aithnichinn lorg do chos,*
> *Och 'us och, mar tha mi 'n nochd*
> *Gur bochd nach d'fhuair mi coir ort.*

> *Tha mo chridhe dhut cho buan,*
> *Ris a' chreag tha 'n grunnd a' chuain,*
> *No comh-ionnan ris an stuaidh*
> *A bhuaileas orr' an comhnuidh.*

He finished the song alone. There was a silence that was almost embarrassing.

"Okay," said the producer, after a pause. "Try another one, number six. The one that doesn't sound like all the others. What's it called?"

"Oran Gillean Alasdair Mhoir," said Archibald, trying to compose and control himself. "Song to the Sons of Big Alexander." Sometimes it's known simply as "The Drowning of the Men."

"Okay," said the producer. "Let's go." But when they were half way through, he said, "Cut, okay, that's enough."

"It's not finished," said Archibald. "It's a narrative."

"That's enough," said the producer.

"You can't cut them like that," said Archibald, "if you do they don't make any sense."

"Look, they don't make any sense to me anyway," said the

producer. "I told you I don't understand the language. We're just rying to gauge audience impact."

Archibald felt himself getting angrier than he felt, perhaps, he should, and he was aware of the looks and gestures from his family. "Be careful," they said , "don't offend him or we won't get the trip."

"Mmmm," he said, rising from his chair and going to the window. Outside, the dusk had turned to dark and the stars seemed to touch the mountain. Although in a room filled with people, he felt very much alone; his mind running silently over the verses of *Mo Chridhe Trom* which had so moved him, moments before.

> *Over lofty mountains lies*
> *The dwelling place of my love,*
> *One whose heart was always warm,*
> *And whom I loved too dearly.*
>
> *And behind the wall of stone*
> *I would recognize your steps,*
> *But how sad am I tonight*
> *Because we're not together.*
>
> *Still my love you will last*
> *Like the rock beneath the sea,*
> *Just as long as will the waves*
> *That strike against it always.*

"Okay, let's call it a night," said the producer. "Thank you all very much. We'll be in touch."

The next morning at nine the producer drove into Archibald's yard. His assistants were with him, packed and ready for Halifax. The assistants remained in the car while the producer, alone, came into Archibald's kitchen. He coughed uncomfortably, and looked about him as if to make sure that they were alone. He reminded Archibald, vaguely, of a nervous father preparing to discuss "the facts of life."

"How were the other groups?" asked Archibald in what he hoped was a non-commital voice.

"The young man, Carver, and his group," said the producer,

"have tremendous *energy*. They have a lot of male voices."

"Mmmm," said Archibald. "What did they sing?"

"I don't remember the names of the song, although I wrote them down. They're packed away. It doesn't matter all that much anyway. They don't know as many songs as you people do though," he concluded.

"No," said Archibald, trying to restrain his sarcasm, "I don't suppose they do."

"Still that doesn't matter so much either, as we only need two or three."

"Mmmm."

"The problem with that group is the way they look."

"The way they *look*?" said Archibald. "Shouldn't it be the way they sing?"

"Not really," said the producer. "See, these performances have a high degree of *visibility*. You're going to be on stage for four nights and the various television networks are all going to be there. This is, in total, a *big show*. It's not a regional show. It will be national and international. It will probably be beamed back to Scotland and Australia and who knows where else. We want people who *look right*, and who will give a good impression of the area and of the province."

Archibald said nothing.

"You see," said the producer. "We've got to have someone we can zoom in on for close-ups — someone who looks the part. We don't want close-ups of people who have had their faces all carved up in brawls."

He continued, "That's why you're so good. You're a great looking man for your age, if you'll pardon me. You're tall and straight and have all your own teeth which helps both your singing and your appearance. You have a *presence*. The rest of your group have nice voices, especially the women, but without you, if you'll pardon me, they're kind of ordinary."

"And then," he added, almost as an afterthought, "there is your reputation. You're known to the folklorists and people like that. You have *credibility*. Very important."

Archibald was aware of Sal's truck coming into the yard and knew that she had seen the producer's car on its way up the mountain.

"Hi," she said, "What's new?"

"I think you're all set but it's up to your grandfather," the producer said.

"What about the MacKenzies?" asked Archibald.

"Garbage. No good at all. An old woman, playing a tape recorder while seven or eight people tried to sing along with it. Wasted our time. We wanted people that were *alive*, not some scratchy tape."

"Mmmm," said Archibald.

"Anyway, you're on. But we'd like a few changes."

"Changes?"

"Yeah, first of all we'll have to cut them. That was what I was trying to get around to last night. You're only going to be on stage for three or four minutes each night and we'd like to get two songs in. They're too long. The other proplem is they're too mournful. Jesus, even the titles, 'My Heart is Heavy,' 'The Drowning of the Men.' Think about it."

"But," said Archibald, trying to sound reasonable, "that's the way those songs are. You've got to hear them in the original way."

"I've got to go now," said Sal. "Got to see about baby sitters and that. See you."

She left in her customary spray of gravel.

"Look," said the producer, "I've got to put on a big show. Maybe you could get some songs from the other group."

"The other group?"

"Yeah," he said, "Carver's. Anyway think about it. I'll call you in about a week and we can really finalize it and work out any other details." And then he was gone.

In the days that followed Archibald *did* think about it. He thought about it more than he had ever thought he would. He thought of the impossibility of trimming the songs and of changing them and he wondered why he seemed the only one in his group who harboured such concerns. Most of the others did not seem very interested when he mentioned it to them, although they did seem interested in shopping lists and gathering the phone numbers of long absent relatives and friends in Halifax.

One evening Carver met Sal on her way to Bingo and told her quite bluntly that he and his group were going.

"No you're not," she said, "we are."

"Wait and see," said Carver. "Look, we need this trip. We need

115

to get a boat engine and we want to buy a truck. You guys are done. Done like a dinner. It matters too much to that Archibald and you're all dependent on him. *Us*, we're *adjustable.*"

"As if we couldn't be adjustable!" said Sal with a laugh as she told of the encounter at their last practice before the anticipated, final phone call. The practice did not go well as far as Archibald was concerned although no one else seemed to notice.

The next day when Archibald, himself, encountered Carver at the general store, down in the valley, he could not resist asking: "What did you sing for that producer fellow?"

"Brochan Lom," said Carver with a shrug.

"Brochan Lom," said Archibald incredulously. Why, that isn't even a song. It's just a bunch of nonsense syllables strung together."

"So what!" said Carver. "He didn't know. No one knows."

"But it's before the Royal Family," said Archibald, surprising even himself at finding such Royalist remnants still within him.

"Look," said Carver wiping his mouth with the back of his hand, " what did the Royal Family ever do for *Me*?"

"Of course people know," said Archibald, pressing on with weary determination. "People in audiences know. Other singers know. Folklorsts know."

"Yeah, maybe so," said Carver with a shrug, "but me I don't know no folklorists."

He looked at Archibald intently for a few seconds and then gathered up his tobacco and left the store.

Archibald was troubled all of that afternoon. He was vaguely aware of his relatives organizing sitters and borrowing suitcases, and, it seemed to him, talking incessantly but saying little. He thought of his conversation with Carver, on the one hand, and strangely enough, he thought of Mrs. MacKenzie on the other. He thought of her with great compassion; she who was probably the best of them all and who had tried the hardest to impress the man from Halifax. The image of her in the twilight of the valley of the MacKenzies, playing the tape recorded voices of her departed family to a man who did not know the language kept running through his mind. He imagined her now, sitting quietly with her knitting needles in her lap, listening to the ghostly voices which were there without their people.

And then that night Archibald had a dream. He had often had

dreams of his wife in the long, long years since her death and had probably brought them on, in the early years, by visiting her grave in the evenings, and sometimes sitting there and talking to her of their hopes and aspirations. And sometimes in the nights following such "conversations" she would come to him and they would talk and touch and sometimes sing. But on this night she sang and only that. She sang with a clarity and a beauty that caused the hairs to rise on the back of his neck even as the tears welled to his eyes. Every note was perfect in its clarity, as perfect and clear as the waiting water droplet hanging on the fragile leaf or the high suspended eagle, outlined against the sky, at the apex of its arc. She sang to him all night until four in the morning when the first rays of morning light began to touch the mountain's top. And then she was gone.

Archibald awoke relaxed and refreshed and at ease in a way that he had seldom felt since sleeping with his wife so many years before. His mind was made up and he was done thinking about it.

Around nine o'clock Sal's truck came into the yard. "That producer fellow is on the phone," she said. "I told him I'd take the message but he wants to talk to you."

"Okay," said Archibald.

In Sal's kitchen the waiting receiver hung and swung from its black spiralated cord.

"Yes, this is Archibald," he said, grasping it firmly. "No I don't think I can get them down to three minutes or speed them up at all. No I don't think so. Yes I have thought about it. Yes I have been in contact with others who sing in my family. No, I don't know about Carver. You'll have to speak to him. Thank-you. Good-bye."

He was aware of the disappointment and grumpiness that spread throughout the house, oozing almost like a rapid ink across a blotter, from where he stood beside the phone. In the next room, he heard a youthful voice say, "All he had to do was shorten the verses in a few stupid, old songs. You'd think he would have done it for *us,* the old coot."

"I'm sorry," he said to Sal, "but I just couldn't do it."

"Do you want a drive home in the truck?" she said.

"No," he said, "never mind, I can walk."

He began to walk up the mountain with an energy and purpose

that reminded him of himself as a younger man. He felt that he was "right" in the way he had felt so many years before when he had courted his future bride and when they had decided to build their house near the mountain's top even though others were coming down. And he felt as he had felt during the short and burning intensity of their too brief lives together. He began, almost, to run.

In the days that followed, Archibald was at peace. One day Sal dropped in and said that Carver was growing a moustache and a beard.

"They told him the moustache would cover his lip and with the beard his scars would be invisible on T.V.," she sniffed. "Makeup will do wonders."

Then one rainy night, after he was finished watching the international and the national and the regional news, Archibald looked out his window. Down on the valley floor he could see the headlights of the cars following the wet pavement of the main highway. People bound for larger destinations who did not know that he existed. And then he noticed one set of lights in particular. They were coming hard and fast along the valley floor and although still miles away they seemed to be coming with a purpose all their own. They "looked" different than the other headlights and in one of those moments of knowledge mixed with intuition Archibald said aloud to himself, "That car is coming here. It is coming for *me.*"

He was rattled at first. He was aware that his decision had caused ill feeling among some members of his family, as well as among various in-laws and others strung out in a far-flung and complicated web of connections he could barely comprehend. He knew also that because of the rain, many of the men had not been in the woods that much lately and were, perhaps spending their time in the taverns talking too much about him and what he had done. He watched as the car swung off the pavement and began its ascent, weaving and sloughing up the mountain in the rain.

Although he was not a violent man, neither did he harbour any illusions about where nor how he lived. "That Archibald," they said, "is nobody's fool." He thought of this now, as he measured the steps to the stove where the giant poker hung. He had had it made by a blacksmith in one of the lumber camps shortly after his marriage. It was of heavy steel and years of poking it into the hot coals of his stove had sharpened its end to a clean and burnished point. When he swung it in his hand, its weight seemed like an ancient sword. He lifted his wooden table easily and placed it at an angle, which he hoped was not too obvious, in the centre of the kitchen, with its length facing the door.

"If they come in the door," he said, "I will be behind the table and in five strides I can reach the poker." He practiced the five strides just to make sure. Then he put his left hand between his legs to adjust himself and straightened his suspenders so that they were perfectly in line. And then he went to the side of the window to watch the coming car.

Because of the recent rains, sections of the ever problematic road had washed away, and at certain places, freshets and small brooks cut across it. Sometimes the rains washed down sand and topsoil as well and the trick was never to accelerate on such washed over sections for fear of being buried in the flowing water and mud. Rather one gunned the motor on the relatively stable sections of the climb (where there was "bottom") and trusted to momentum to get across the streams. Archibald watched the progress of the car. Sometimes he lost its headlights because of his perspective and the trees, but only momentarily. As it climbed, swerving back and forth, the wet branches slapping and briefly silhouetted against its headlights, Archibald began to read the dark wet roadway in his own mind. And he also began to read the driver's reflexes, as he swung out from the gullies and then in close to the mountain's wall. He began almost to admire the driver. "Whoever that is," he said, "is very drunk but also very good."

The car hooked and turned into his yard without any apparent change in speed, its headlights flashing on his house and through his window. Archibald moved behind his table and stood, tall and balanced and ready. Before the sound of the slamming car door faded, his own kitchen door seemed to blow in and Carver stood there unsteadily, blinking in the light with the rain blowing at his back and dripping off his beginning beard.

"Yeah," he said over his shoulder, "he's here, bring it in."

Archibald waited, his eyes intent upon Carver but also sliding sideways to his poker.

They came into his porch and there were five of them, carrying boxes.

"Put them on the floor, here," said Carver, indicating a space just acoss the threshold. "And try not to dirty his floor."

Archibald knew then he would be all right and moved out from behind his table.

"Open the boxes," said Carver to one of the other men. The boxes were filled with forty ounce bottles of liquor. It was as if someone were preparing for a wedding.

"These are for you," said Carver. "We bought them at a bootleggers two hours ago. We been away all day. We been to Glace Bay and to New Waterford and we were in a fight in the parking lot at the tavern in Bras D'Or, and a couple of us got banged up pretty bad. Anyway, not much to say."

Archibald looked at them, framed in the doorway leading to his porch. There was no mystery about the kind of day they had had, even if Carver had not told him. Even now, one of them, a tall young man was rocking backward on his heels, almost literally falling asleep on his feet as he stood in the doorway. There was a fresh cut on Carver's temple which could not be covered by either his moustache nor his beard. Archibald looked at all the liquor and was moved by the total inappropriateness of the gift; bringing all of this to him, the most abstemious man on the mountain. Somehow it moved him even more. And he was aware of its cost in many ways.

He almost envied them their closeness and their fierceness and what the producer fellow had called their tremendous energy. And he imagined it was men like they, who had given, in their recklessness, all they could think of in that confused and stormy past. Going with their claymores and the misunderstood language of their warcries to "perform" for the Royal Families of the past. But he was not sure of that either. He smiled at them and gave a small nod of acknowledgement. He did not know quite what to say.

"Look," said Carver, with that certainty that marked everything he did.

"Look Archibald, *We know,* we *really know.*"

R.J. MacSween / Glace Bay

Born in North Sydney, Father MacSween now lives in Antigonish where he teaches English at St. Francis Xavier University. For many years he was the editor of **The Antigonish Review** whose pages have included many of the finest writers in North America. The following poems are exerpts from **The Forgotten World,** and **Double Shadows.** R.J. MacSween has published two other volumes: **the secret city,** and **Furiously Wrinkled.**

I was born in 1915 at North Sydney, N.S., and spent the next five years of life on a farm in Ironville, Cape Breton, a part of the district of Boisdale. My memories of those years are very precious to me and seem more real than later events of my life when I was more aware of my surroundings. At that early age I lived as through my skin, my sense of the environment was so keen and so hungry. Nevertheless, the concrete memories of that time are few and consist for the most part of flashes from the past into the more active arena of the present.

When I was five, we moved permanently to Glace Bay and there lived on the edge of town. Our state was still rural, the woods came right up to the back fence, but the animals were gone. The coal mines and the machine shops near the center of town soon became a normal part of my life. Later on as an adult, I was to spend five years in New Waterford, another mining community of the same type.

In 1948 I became a professor of English at St. Francis Xavier in Antigonish. What I thought would be a short stay has lengthened into thirty-five years. Still, there is no doubt about my Cape Breton allegiance. My early years have given me an indelible stamp, and no span of time away from Cape Breton could ever erase it. So be it.

LONG SWORDS

the Celts had long swords
for duel and for battle
we can imagine their stance
   legs wide apart
   braced firmly
   like an overeager golfer
we can see the muscles strain
   agony on the face
left arm in the shield
   right arm swinging the avenger
   at a shrinking enemy

it was not so with warriors
   who fought at close quarters
   and aimed at complete destruction
the Roman sword was short
    could annihilate ten
   to the Celts' one
the Roman stopped the long sword
   with the shield's edge
   then stabbed quickly
   for the face
his equipment was developed
   from the gladiator's
in the arena warm with blood and sweat
he learned all the tricks
   whereby man can survive
   against enemies
   as skilled and as desperate
   as himself

and so it is with everyone
   of his type and caliber
at a distance they are helpless to destroy
   but close at hand
     they can extract one's life
     without delay or bungling
     and in their hands
     the knives
     can scarcely be seen

R.J. MacSween

SMALL FIRE

I live for this hour
    not aeons to come
each morning I swear
    I shall not succumb

let others aspire
    to the sun in the sky
I tend my small fire
    for fear it should die

I'll make my face stone
    to the shadow death's made
to a corner alone
    I'll banish that shade

which grows in the night
    a tree thick with fear
but my fire leaps with light
    all the nights of the year

R.J. MacSween

OUR GARDEN

we have carried our garden
   into a country
   where all the flowers wither
our very thoughts decay
   in this acid air
blossoms that made the prophets
   leap for joy
   drop their petals in the dust

we have carried our God
   into this furnace
the eyes smart
the skin dries
God has become a withered man
   a leather idol
   fallen to one side

we must drop all our belongings
   and move to another land
the way is long
   our perseverance small
take nothing from the parched land
   that has betrayed us
across the mountains
   in moist valleys
   we will rediscover
     our history

R.J. MacSween

Farley Mowat / River Bourgeois

Farley Mowat has sold over ten million copies of his books in 22 languages. He is perhaps best known for his non-fiction: **People of the Deer, The Desperate People,** and **Sibir** to name a few. His short fiction was collected in **The Snow Walker** and he has written two books, **A Whale for the Killing** and **Never Cry Wolf,** that have been turned into major motion pictures.

Born in Ontario, Mowat moved around with his family as a child and developed a legendary passion for nature and the arctic in particular. In 1949 he began writing for a living and while much of his work has concerned animals, the arctic and adventure, he has established himself as one of the most skillful of autobiographers in Canada. **And No Birds Sang** is an account of Mowat's experiences in World War II. In a forthcoming book, **Sea of Slaughter,** he returns to an examination of man's impact on the natural environment. It looks at "animate creation as it was in the Gulf of St. Lawrence region c. 1500 during the first European contact, and the disasters that have overwhelmed it since." Mowat lives near River Bourgeois with his wife, Claire, who is also a writer.

> *What do I think of Cape Breton Island? I think so much of it that I've chosen to live there over any other place on earth I've ever seen. Not for the scenery, but for the quality of its people. They are survivors, and that puts them in a special category in this world of ours.*

Snow

by Farley Mowat

When Man was still very young he had already become aware that certain elemental forces dominated the world womb. Embedded on the shores of their warm sea, the Greeks defined these as Fire and Earth and Air and Water. But at first the Greek sphere was small and circumscribed and the Greeks did not recognize the fifth elemental.

About 330 B.C., a peripatetic Greek mathematician named Pytheas made a fantastic voyage northward to Iceland and into the Greenland Sea. Here he encountered the fifth elemental in all of its white and frigid majesty, and when he returned to the warm blue Mediterranean, he described what he had seen as best he could. His fellow countrymen concluded he must be a liar since even their vivid imaginations could not conceive of the splendour and power inherent in the white substance that sometimes lightly cloaked the mountain homes of their high-dwelling Gods.

Their failure to recognize the immense power of snow was not entirely their fault. We who are the Greeks' inheritors have much the same trouble comprehending its essential magnitude.

How do *we* envisage snow?

It is the fragility of Christmas dreams sintering through azure darkness to the accompaniment of the sound of sleigh bells.

It is the bleak reality of a stalled car and spinning wheels impinging on the neat time schedule of our self-importance.

It is the invitation that glows ephemeral on a woman's lashes on a winter night.

It is the resignation of suburban housewives as they skin wet snowsuits from runny-nosed progeny.

It is the sweet gloss of memory in the failing eyes of the old as they recall the white days of childhood.

It is the banality of a TV advertisement pimping Coca Cola on a snowbank at Sun Valley.

It is the gentility of utter silence in the muffled heart of a snow-clad forest.

It is the brittle wind-rush of skis; and the bellicose chatter of snowmobiles.

Snow is these things to us, together with many related images; yet all deal only with obvious aspects of a multifaceted, kaleidoscopic and protean element.

Snow, which on our planet is a phoenix continually born again from its own dissolution, is also a galactic and immortal presence. In the nullity of outer space, clouds of snow crystals, immeasurably vast, drift with time, unchanged since long before our world was born, unchangeable when it will be gone. For all that the best brains of science and the sharpest of the cyclopean eyes of astronomers can tell, the glittering crystals flecking the illimitable void are as one with those that settle on our hands and faces out of the still skies of a December night.

Snow is a single flake caught for an instant on a windowpane. But it is also a signboard in the solar system. When astronomers peer up at Mars they see the Red Planet as a monochromatic globe - except for its polar caps from which gleaming mantles spread toward the equatorial regions. As the antelope flashes its white rump on the dun prairies, so does Mars signal to worlds beyond it with the brilliance of our common sun reflected from its plains of snow.

And so does Earth.

When the first star voyager arcs into deep space, he will watch the greens and blues of our seas and lands dissolve and fade as the glove diminishes until the last thing to beacon the disappearing Earth will be the glare of our own polar heliographs. Snow will be the last of the elementals of his distant eye. Snow may provide the first shining glimpse of our world to inbound aliens ... if they have eyes with which to see.

Snow is crystalline dust, tenuous amongst the stars; but on Earth it is, in yet another guise, the Master Titan. To the South it holds the entire continent of Antarctica in absolute thrall. To the north it crouches heavily upon mountain ranges and the island subcontinent of Greenland literally sags and sinks beneath its weight. For glaciers are but another guise of snow.

Glaciers are born while the snow falls; fragile, soft and almost disembodied . . . but falling steadily without a thawing time. Years pass, decades, centuries, and the snow falls. Now there is weight where there was none. At the surface of an undulating white waste, there seems to be no alteration, but in the frigid depths the crystals are deformed; they change in structure, interlock with increasing intimacy and eventually melt into black, lightless ice.

Four times during Earth's most recent geological age snow fell like this across much of the northern half of our continent and in Europe and Asia too. Each time, snow altered the face of almost half a world. A creeping glacial nemesis as much as two miles thick oozed outward from vast central domes, excoriating the planet's face, stripping it of life and soil, ripping deep wounds into the primordial rock and literally depressing Earth's stone mantle hundreds of feet below its former level. The snow fell, softly, steadily, until countless millions of tons of water had vanished from the seas, locked up within the glaciers; and the seas themselves withdrew from the edges of the continents.

There is no natural phenomenon known to us that can surpass the dispassionate power of a great glacier. The rupturing of Earth during its most appalling earthquake cannot compare with it. The raging water of the seas in their most violent moments cannot begin to match it. Air, howling in the dementia of hurricanes, is nothing beside it. The inner fire that blows a mountain to pieces and inundates the surrounding plains with floods of flaming lava is weak by comparison.

A glacier is the macrocosmic form of snow. But in its microscopic forms, snow epitomizes ethereal beauty. It is a cliche to say that no two snowflakes are identical, but it is a fact that each single snowflake that has fallen throughout all of time, and that will fall through what remains of time, has been - will be - a unique creation in symmetry and form.

I know of one man who has devoted most of his adult life to the study of this transient miracle. He has built a special house fitted with a freezing system, instead of heating equipment. It is a house with a gaping hole in its roof. On snowy days and nights he sits in icy solitude catching the falling flakes on plates of pre-chilled glass and hurriedly photographing them through an enlarging lens. For him the fifth elemental in its infinite diversity and singularity is beauty incarnate, and a thing to worship.

Few of us would be of a mind to share his almost medieval passion. In truth, modern man has insensibly begun to develop a schizophrenic attitude toward the fifth elemental. Although we may remember our childhood experience of it with nostalgia, more and more we have begun to think of snow with enmity. We cannot control snow, nor bend it to our will. The snow that fell harmlessly and beneficiently upon the natural world our forefathers lived in has the power to inflict chaos on the mechanical new world we have been building. A heavy snowfall in New York, Montreal, Chicago, produces a paralytic stroke. Beyond the congealed cities it chokes the arteries of our highways, blocks trains, grounds aircraft, fells power and telephone cables. Even a moderate snowfall causes heavy inconvenience - if smashed cars, broken bodies, and customers for the undertakers are only inconvenciences.

We will probably come to like snow even less. Stories about the good old-fashioned winters when snow mounted to the eaves of houses and horse-hauled sleighs were galloped over drifts at tree-top level are not just old wives' tales. A hundred years ago such happenings were commonplace. However, during the past century our climate has experienced a warming trend, an upswing (from our point of view), in the erratic cyclic variations of the weather. It has probably been a short-term swing and the downswing may soon be upon us. And where will we be then, poor things, in our delicately structured artificial world? Will we still admire snow? More likely we will curse the very word.

However, when that time comes there may still be men alive who will be unperturbed by the gentle, implacable downward drift. They are the true people of the snows.

They live only in the northern hemisphere because the realm of snow in the southern hemisphere - Antarctica - will not permit the existence of any human life unless equipped with a panoply of protective devices not far short of what a spaceman needs. The snow people ring the North Pole. They are the Aleuts, Eskimos and Athabascan Indians of North America; the Greenlanders; the Lapps, Nensi, Chukchee, Yakuts, Yukagirs and related peoples of Eurasia and Siberia.

Cocooned in the machine age, we smugly assume that because

these people live unarmoured by our ornate technology, they must lead the most marginal kind of existence, faced with so fierce a battle to survive that they have no chance to realize the "human potential." Hard as it may strike into our dogmatic belief that technology offers the only valid way of life, I can testify from my own experiences with many of the snow people that this assumption is wrong. They mostly lived good lives, before our greed and our megolomaniac arrogance impelled us to meddle in their affairs. That is, if it be good to live at peace with oneself and one's fellow men, to be in harmony with one's environment, to laugh and love without restraint, to know fulfilment in one's daily life, and to rest from birth to death upon a sure and certain pride.

Snow was these people's ally. It was their protection and their shelter from abysmal cold. Eskimos built complete houses of snow blocks. When heated only with simple animal-oil lamps, these had comfortable interior temperatures, while outside the wind screamed unheard and the mercury dropped to fifty degrees or more below zero. Compacted snow provides nearly perfect insulation. It can be cut and shaped much more easily than wood. It is light to handle and strong, if properly used. A snowhouse with an inner diameter of twenty feet and a height of ten feet can be built by two men in two hours. On special occasions Eskimos used to build snowhouses fifty feet in diameter and, by linking several such together, formed veritable snow mansions.

All of the snow people use snow for shelter in one way or another. If they are sedentary folk possessing wooden houses they bank their homes with thick snow walls in wintertime. Some dig a basement in a snowdrift and roof it with reindeer skins. As long as snow is plentiful, the peoples of the far north seldom suffer serious discomfort from the cold.

Snow also makes possible their transportation system. With dog sleds and reindeer sleds, or afoot on snowshoes, or trail skis, they can travel almost anywhere. The whole of the snow world becomes a highway. They can travel at speed, too. A dog or reindeer team can move at twenty miles an hour and easily cover a hundred miles a day.

The mobility snow gives them, combined with the way snow modifies the behaviour of game animals, ensures that - other things being equal - the snow people need not go hungry. Out on the Arctic ice a covering of snow gives the seals a sense of false security. They make breathing holes in the ice, roofed by a thin layer of snow. The Chukchee or Eskimo hunter finds these places and waits beside them until, at a signal from a tell-tale wand of ivory or wood inserted in the roof, he plunges his spear down into the unseen animal below.

In wooded country, moose, elk and deer are forced by deep snow to "yard" in constricted areas where they can be killed nearly as easily as cattle in a pen. Most important of all, every animal, save those with wings and those who live beneath the snow, leaves tracks upon its surface. From bears to hares they become more vulnerable to the human hunter as soon as the first snow coats the land.

The snow people know snow as they know themselves. In these days our scientists are busy studying the fifth elemental, not so much out of scientific curiosity but because we are anxious to hasten the rape of the north or fear we may have to fight wars in the lands of snow. With vast expenditures of time and money, the scientists have begun to separate the innumerable varieties of snow and to give them names. They could have saved themselves the trouble. Eskimos have more than a hundred compound words to express different varieties and conditions of snow. The Lapps have almost as many. Yukagir reindeer herdsmen on the Arctic coast of Siberia can tell the depth of snow cover, its degree of compactness, and the amount of internal ice cyrstallization it contains simply by glancing at the surface.

The northern people are happy when snow lies heavy on the land. They welcome the first show in autumn, and often regret its passing in the spring. Snow is their friend. Without it they would have perished or - almost worse from their point of view - they would long since have been driven south to join us in our frenetic rush to wherever it is that we are bound.

Somewhere, on this day, the snow is falling. It may be sifting thinly on the cold sands of a desert, spreading a strange pallidity and flecking the dark, upturned faces of a band of Semitic nomads. For them it is in the nature of a miracle; and it is certainly an omen and they are filled with awe and chilled with apprehension.

It may be whirling fiercely over the naked sweep of frozen plain in the Siberian steppe, or on the Canadian prairies, obliterating summer landmarks, climbing in scimitar drifts to wall up doors and windows of farmhouses. Inside, the people wait in patience. While the blizzard blows, they rest; when it is over, work will begin again. And in the spring the melted snows will water the new growth springing out of the black earth.

It may be settling in great flakes on a calm night over a vast city; spinning cones of distorted vision in the headlights of creeping cars and covering the wounds, softening the suppurating ugliness inflicted on the earth by modern man. Children hope it will continue all night long so that no buses, street cars or family automobiles will be able to carry the victims off to school in the morning. But adult men and women wait impatiently, for if it does not stop soon the snow will smother the intricate designs that have been ordained for the next day's pattern of existence.

Or the snow may be slanting swiftly down across a cluster of tents huddled below a rock ridge on the arctic tundra. Gradually it enfolds a pack of dogs who lie, noses thrust under bushy tails, until the snow covers them completely and they sleep warm. Inside the tents men and women smile. Tomorrow the snow may be deep enough and hard enough so that the tents can be abandoned and the welcome domes of snowhouses can rise again to turn winter into a time of gaiety, of songs, of leisure and lovemaking.

Somewhere the snow is falling.

Ellison Robertson / Scotch Lake

Ellison Robertson was born in 1947 and grew up in various communities in industrial Cape Breton. He attended the Nova Scotia College of Art and Design and worked for two years in the college gallery. His paintings have appeared in a number of shows in Cape Breton and at Dresden Galleries in Halifax. In 1980, Robertson illustrated **Songs and Stories of Deep Cove** and in 1981 published **A Sketchbook of Cape Breton.** His stories have appeared in **The Antigonish Review, Chezzetcook,** and **The Pottersfield Portfolio.** He continues to paint and is currently illustrating a book of Gaelic folk tales. A novel is forthcoming. "Cranberry Head" appears here in print for the first time.

Ellison Robertson lives and works at Scotch Lake, twelve miles from Sydney.

> *Leaving Cape Breton has always been a way of coming closer to home. In ten years of art school, travel and work away from the island, I was often reminded that I was a Cape Bretoner. Usually this meant a realization of the story telling, humour and vitality of the place but often too it was a negative definition made by others who accepted a myth of drunkeness, violence, some sort of isolated inferiority ensconced, oddly enough, in a surpassingly beautiful setting. I was offended even, especially, when I was seen as an exception because I was an artist or because I could talk about books. But there was a line on that too. 'Thousands of Cape Bretoners had left to rise to success in commerce, government and so on' (bettering themselves apparently). Well, it's probably true, but an even greater number remained to sustain a wide community of various origins, to work and struggle at the heart of the fight between labour and capital. The very genius of radicalism had flourished here.*

Cranberry Head

by Ellison Robertson

Say Jack Say Jack Say Jack Sayjack sayjack sayjacksayjack . . .

Two sets of rails: The one unused, dull rusted: The other used, polished, sun glinting.

Sayjacksayjack . . . The black, oiled wheels turn slow, then fast for the half mile run, then slow again, braking in the dark ruined complexity of the wash plant where uniformed company police await any of us too slow in jumping from the coal cars; fat men moving with their only haste of the day, vicious, furious if you're caught; their black, polished, steel-toed boots seeking connection with any of us unlucky or slow enough to get caught. Red contorted faces mouth their threats, "Get the Jesus out . . . Kick your arse for you." Their names for us, "Little Bastards . . . Little Pricks . . ." Our names for them, "Tub of Guts . . . No Arse . . . Nose the Rose . . ." Nose the Rose has a great purple veined face, a great purple bulb throbbing at its center. He'll die one day chasing us. He'll explode one of these days. Yeah, a great purple nose exploding against a laughing, running boy's head; fury scalding you, running down your back . . .

No Arse is the one to watch, the one to fear. He's younger than the rest, a short skinny bugger, can outrun most of us. And if he catches you he doesn't kick you, he doesn't slap you, he takes you back to their little brick office, sits you on top of a high stool and shakes his head at you, so short it's level with your own, and if you're stupid enough to give it, he writes your name in a book, and he talks about criminals and thieves and calls you sneaky. "What'll your father think of you? . . . Won't your mother be ashamed?" Things a teacher would say to you. Then he leaves you sitting on that stool while he looks out the grimy glass of the door or moves papers around on the small table and if he goes out he locks the door and after a long time he takes you in the Company's black coal grimed car and drives to your house and says again to your mother all the things about sneaking thieves and some mothers listen nodding and others curse him out of their house and once when he took Wayne Olden home his father was there and it was No Arse who was kicked out of the yard. We know that and he knows we do and he tries harder than ever to catch us.

I know all this from the others . . . he's never caught me though he's tried. Our neighbour, Mr. Olden, said to me too, "Those long legs boy are a curse and you don't know it . . . you'll always be quicker to run than to stand and fight."

Sayjack . . . say-jack . . . when the train is moving slowly past , I lie against the slope of the slag dump and wait. If we run to the train too soon the stoker will jump from the engine to chase us with his shovel or a man may run from the end of the train if we wait too long. The men on the train never catch us, don't really try. It is like a rule in a game but it changes enough so we always have to be careful. Once they stopped the train when we were already on top of the cars and all of them, even the engineer, came running to curse at us and kick wildly at anyone near enough.

The sun beat strong on the neck and along the legs. The ground cooler, still warm against face and hands. Grey packed ground, black flecked with slate and coal. Stomach sick with waiting and the no earth smell of the dumps.

Rolled burlap bags, tucked in belts, hard against bellies.

Now.

Everyone is there but you are alone as you run toward the moving train . . . sayjacksayjacksayjack . . . the wheel rail sound comes faster to my ears and the train judged to be moving slowly seems to be moving faster faster faster. Ladders are clasped, footholds found, the left foot dragging a moment in the gravel and cinder. Made it. And now the others are there again, climbing above you or still on the moving ground and needing a hand.

The rocking cars. The sound now barely audible above your own blood's pounding, your breath quick with effort, but the sounds are still there. The engine stack echoes JACK JACK JACK . . . the wheels recognize the climbing boys . . . Dougie John Dougie John . . . Mar tin tin tin . . .

On the top of the loose sliding coal scrabbling with feet and hands to send showers of black shining coal to the ground now whirring past. We glance up frequently to judge the distance to the washplant. We have to jump before we are close enough to get caught. The train will be moving faster than when we jumped on. There will be cuts and bruises and always a moment of suspended motion, the gasping for breath to run before the blue uniforms come jolting along from the shadow of the tin, rusting buildings.

The one who jumps off first is the coward for the day, bullied by everyone else. It is usually Wayne who leaps down in a panic. Dougie Miller is always last but he is older and even the company cops avoid grabbing him. He will strike back.

Get off now. Feet sink in the shifting coal. Hands gone black and slippery with sweat and coal seek the rungs of a ladder. Eyes watch alternately for the cops and for the piece of blurring ground that will recognize you and tug you down into a rolling encounter like running against a wall.

But leaping now I hang for a long drawn moment with a confusing image fixed shakily in my eyes. We've all jumped except Martin. Martin is clawing the sky, still upright on top of the diminishing pile of coal scattering down from the car's edge.

My breath is gone. I forgot to land running, to roll on impact. My face is burning. They're going to catch me. I struggle to my feet. My companions stand in a ragged line beside the train which I realize has stopped. We stare, not understanding, not running, not fearing pursuit.

The uniformed men, the engineer and the stoker are all in a group staring back at us. Tub of Guts is kneeling by the tracks . . . Nose the Rose is running towards the small brick office and No Arse begins shouting but still not moving toward us. "You bastards . . . which one? You bastards . . . all of you . . . which one? This boy . . . you'll pay . . ."

It's Martin
I saw . . . he fell
Nobody . . . was close to him
I saw . . . all blood, gagging and shaking on the ground
He had a fit everyone knows he has fits
I seen him lots of times
Nobody's fault that No Arse bastard
His arm all blood

Finally a couple of the cops step out of their shock and move our way but we are gone running desperately, forgetting our burlap sacks, forgetting to gather up the coal, running for home, each of us alone.

* * *

The sinks of nearly all the houses in Cranberry emptied into the slop drains, deep ditches patterning the empty ground behind the rows of houses on the four streets, and flowing sluggishly into one of the two ponds on the headland.

A favourite form of bullying consisted of grabbing someone during a game and hurling him into the heavy grey slime of one of these troughs.

* * *

'Where, though?"

"Away honey, please, I've told you. Daddy is far away working at a job where we can't go and he'll be back as soon, as soon, as he can . . ."

"Daddy . . . away . . . job . . . we can't . . . as soon as soon . . ." Mattie mouths, staring at our mother's face to see this is the truth.

But it is not. I know. I never ask because I know. I share the secret with my mother but I'm not exactly sure what the secret is, not exactly . . . just that the truth is a lie. My mother never lies but this time it is all right.

"Look after your mother," he said. "You're the man while I'm gone. You're almost nine. Look after your sisters and your brother too."

Now I am almost ten.

* * *

A flat marshy headland, beaches on either side, broken sandstone and slate cliffs rising where the point noses into the Atlantic, where the colliery workings are massed against the sea and sky, slightly higher than any other portion of Cranberry Head, dominating every potential view, but just there after a while with no need to think about it.

* * *

"Eii-ahh-kei... eii-ahh-kei..."

"Eli-ahh-kei," you call back to the dark. "Can I got out Mom?"

Eii-ahh-kei is Joey's invention, part of our secret code. It means, Come to meet a friend, or sometimes when we are out playing, I am here and where are you?

Out into the damp breathing dark. Trembling clouds of mosquitoes move across the outside light, engulf your head like a vast steamy palm, fingering your blinking eyes, clotting ears and nose when you come too close to the drains, invisible but stinking in the summer night.

Eii...where is he...ahh...always a little knot of doubt before I step from the circle of light to the all dark dark dark... kei...what if Penny was out here...close to the house, could call out MOM...if it is Penny...never thought of it before... change the code...if its Joey tell him change...

"What you doin'?"

A small crouching figure...my eyes wide in concentration find him, sweeping away a few layers of the dark. It's Wayne.

"Nothing." He looks at the ground, always shy, always afraid. Momma's Boy. Momma's Boy, they chant after him when his whining frustration breaks out during games. I've seen him, hurt, lying on the ground clutching the hurting arm or leg or head, squeezing out scalding tears so easily, crying, O Mommy O Daddy O Mommy O Daddy O . . . Oblivious. Awakening sympathy always turns to disgust. When the wind blows his mother keeps him home, afraid her little Wayne will blow away.

"What do you want?"

"Nothin'...what you doin'?"

"Nothing, I was having some tea."

"Ma won't let me...what could we do?"

"I don't know...look for Joey or something?"

"I'm not...not allowed to leave the yard."

"Maybe I'll go in."

"Don't you wanta do something?"

"We could go in the club."

Go around the house in silence to the front yard. Light from the electric pole scattered dim by the sullen poplars. A front porch, disused, walled in half-way up so I put a roof across that and a

fourth wall with a hinged door; a clubhouse.
"There's a candle.
"I don't have a match."
"Me either, we could read some comics if we had a match."
"You got some?"
"You know. Here in a box." Reaching round the formless dark.
"Why are you pushing me?"
"I'm looking for the box, can't find it."
"Gone maybe."
"Stolen maybe . . ."
"Who?"
"Maybe you?"
"No. Oh no, I wouldn't . . . I know a joke . . . Fella went to get his boat and there she was . . . gone."
"That's funny, Wayne, if it wasn't your boat or if it wasn't your comics."
"Ahh . . ."
"Shh . . . what's that?"
"What?"
"That, someone laughing . . . shouting, let's see."
The night has a soft glow after the darker clubhouse. Sound guiding now, eyes peering about uselessly. Until I see them. Three boys on the road near the rail crossing, beneath the yellow light of an electric pole.
"Let's see what they're doing."
Wayne stays back under the trees. "I can't leave the yard."
"Just up through the shortcut . . . you can see your door, hear your mother . . . ahh come on Wayne." A sudden unbearable, restlessness, impatience with Wayne, with slow stupid summer nights, itching at you worse than all the mosquitoes. "They've got a dummy . . . come on." I move along to the road while Wayne drags along behind me.
"I can't leave the yard, can't."
"Don't be scared all the time."
"Ma said . . ."
"Ma said Ma said Ma said . . . just half way up . . . we'll sneak up and watch them." I crossed the road, jumped the ditch and moved along the path worn in the coarse grass bordering the dumps. I glance back every so often to see Wayne moving along behind, stopping and looking nervously at his house again and

again. His hesitation irritates me more and more, making me bolder. I crouch finally in the grass where they won't see me. Wayne comes up close behind. The three boys are Dougie Miller, his brother Walter and another boy named Brian something. They had a dummy tied to a string. They would prop it against a pole then yank it into the headlights of any car that came along. They jerked the dummy toward them in the tall grass where they'd hidden. Most drivers slammed on their brakes as this human apparition staggered into the light. They'd realize in a moment what the trick was, curse at the hidden boys, or some maybe secretly laughing at the memory of themselves in the tall face prickling grass, dizzy with suppressed laughter. Anyone who got out of his car saw only the retreating forms of three laughing boys, a fourth lifeless figure tossing along in their flight.

No cars came for some time. I am going to go back home, bored now with all of this but when we stand up Wayne shouts, "What are you doing?"

"Jesus!" Startled, the three look about, not sure where to react but slowly realizing the high cracking sound that was Wayne's voice. They look at us. "Who is it?"

"Jackie." It is Wayne who calls my name. I stare at him, his face a blur against the night. "And Wayne," he adds then at half volume.

"You want to play?"

"Naw..."

"Come on..."

"We better go..." Wayne whispers, pleading.

"You go." I say, sick of him. I walk up to the three waiting boys. "Who made the dummy?"

"Which dummy, Dummy?"

They knock me down. Now I am standing again. They hit me. Arms hold me. I hate my own stupidity. I feel so tired. I was flailing, biting. I can hear Wayne shouting something but I seem to have seen him already running away across the dumps. My skin is burning all over. I was lying down again, alone. I can hear someone shouting, but it makes no sense. I stand up. I'm not alone. The dummy's blank face is turned skyward next to where I'd lain.

"You and me dummy... you... me." I walk home, the ground seeming to jar with each step. I am crying, my nose running. I wipe a hand across my face. In the light a black smear on my hand I know must be blood. I can hear Wayne now saying over and over, where he stands at the end of the driveway, "I told you . . . I said we shouldn't have gone . . . I told you."

"Please stop." I feel sick. My voice is strange.

"I told you . . ."

I hit his face and he stops, too startled even to cry for a moment. His nose bleeds, his shocked face a mirror to mine. Now he clutches his face, beginning "O Mommy O Daddy O Mommy O" as he runs for his house.

"I'm sorry . . . I'm sorry . . . I'm sorry . . ." I say over and over as I stumble along toward my door not knowing who I am apologizing to. But maybe to my Mother when her pale face finally turns to see mine as I carry it into the kitchen like an insult.

* * *

We came in a taxi. My Mother paid the driver and led us to the door of the new house. There was a padlock but she had a key, as if she had been here before. I helped push the door open, all of us jumping back as it gave a squawk and swung open to hit the wall with an echoing thud. My Mother let her eyes go wide with a funny look and we all laughed. Our new house.

Mattie, Ann and John stayed close to Mother who moved across the kitchen as if she were looking for something. The room was empty except for a sink and a coal stove. She opened all the windows. The house smelled sour wet like a cellar but now the smell was blown away. I stayed near the door without knowing why . . . our laughter of a moment ago a distant sound. Mattie left the kitchen and was back in a minutes saying excitedly, "Jackie, there's colored windows upstairs, come see. All red, all blue, all green."

I felt sleepily indifferent to everything. I wanted to climb into my bed but my bed was in a truck somewhere on the road we'd taken in the taxi. I thought I would sit on the step in the warm morning sun but when I turned around I saw the yard had been silently surrounded by children of various ages: all watching.

"Jack?" My Mother spoke just above a whisper.

I glanced at her and closed the door on the brilliant staring faces.

* * *

The mothers never left the houses except to hang the clothes on the line or to catch a bus for uptown. No family had more than one car unless an older son living at home bought one. I never saw a woman drive one of these cars, indeed some men would drive the few hundred yards to the mine's parking lot where the cars sat untouched for an entire shift unless by some aerial-snapping boys pointlessly wandering among the dark, bulky Fords, Chevys and Plymouths.

My mother went to sit on the beach when we wanted to swim. No other adults did at first but a few other women joined her after a few weeks. Then she came with us only every second time, every third time, now and then and finally only if we insisted. She still feared for us at large, but I think she began to fear more the company of the gossiping women probing her exile.

The mothers seemed to be fearful of everything outside their cloistered kitchens. Don't go near the tracks . . . near the cliffs . . . near the deep water of the point . . . near the ponds . . . near the forts . . . and don't, don't, don't go near the pit. The rules were too comprehensive not to transgress.

* * *

The corruption of frost ruined apples (the waste of a barrel left in an unheated porch far into October offending even an eight year old) released a sad sour smell by fingers dissolving ice where they pressed firm the barrel rim to draw in the hurt of cold.

My mother and father embraced, murmuring words I could not hear or could not understand. Mattie sat at the kitchen table crying but only because she was told to stay inside and the door was firmly shut. And I was crouched in the sick smelling space between the apple barrel and the frost coated wall, crouched and hidden I must have thought, but my parents separated and my father lifted me up and said, "Look after your mother . . . you're the man while I' gone . . . you're almost nine . . . look after your sisters and your brother too." And smiled at me, then smiled at my mother, as if he were the only one that didn't know there was anything wrong, and even smiled at the policeman outside who had everyone's attention now while he cleared his throat and stepped onto the bottom step and sent a long white plume of breath in our direction as he spoke but averted his face from us before he finished so the plume shifted direction too and my eyes followed it and stayed staring at the blue sky while I listened to him say, "I guess we better get going."

They were gone. My mother stood on the steps, her arms clasped against the cold, shivering but not crying and I stepped into the kitchen feeling nothing but the sharp breath-stopping lump in my throat. Mattie looked at me sullenly then went on crying; I knew I should comfort her but thought, she's too young to even know what's happening. I heard myself shouting, "Shut up your stupid crying!" and ran upstairs to my room to push my face into a pillow while a pointless, stupid rage burned at the rims of my unseeing eyes.

* * *

Nearly everyone walked uptown to school but when it rained, when it turned too cold, almost everyone took the bus. I had been living in Cranberry four months but I was still the new guy. I got on the bus and the only seats were at the back where the biggest boys sat. They opened a window and dropped me out onto the ground. I boarded the bus again and the process was repeated. I stood at the open door again and the driver smiled at me but it seemed a smile of complicity reflecting the smirking faces straining to see me from the rear of the bus; I walked to school in the rain.

* * *

The children were: Ella, thick limbed barrel, the shadow of her obese mother, older than any of us, the object of so much ridicule to which she never rose but endured with stolid, mute patience till she was sixteen and prompty left school, and disappeared into her house (large and squat as it's inhabitants) to be seen only rarely moving with slow, difficult purpose to the bus stop or the co-op . . . no one jeered at her now for she'd left her tormented childhood and tipped into the adult world; Martin, who had hair so white he could have been an albino but his eyes were a dull green and it would have been too much to add one more affliction

to this slight, spidery figure, who was an epileptic, who was prone to every illness, who lost an arm to a train in circumstances we all falsified, yet struggled to be at the center of every game, running, swimming, climbing as well as anyone who was whole; he was immune to teasing, sometimes lost in his own mysterious thoughts, and always open to be bribed to fake a fit which would halt a class for half an hour; Wayne, O Mommy O Daddy O Mommy O . . . Joey, a few years older than me, separable from me only by his strange introverted disappearing acts, thought by some adults to be simple minded though I knew him as an eccentric genius and comic imagination, aloof to everyone but me and protected by his families peculiar status as oddballs and also as farming residents on the headland as long or longer than any of the miner's families had been there, and Joey, whose thoughts fed on the great world beyond his, would never leave here but live in the family house after all of the family was dead or moved away, would eventually marry, work as a milkman or part-time mechanic self-taught, would have many children and grow yearly more vague, dreamier, till he resembled his wry sinewy old man; Russel, a redhead whose hawk nose always dripped a suspended green gob, drooping then withdrawn to the rhythm of his speech, who was the champion of every physical endeavour, large for his age (13), sometimes working on a fishing boat during the summer, drinking, smoking, swearing, he seemed a leader though he seldom condescended to spend time among us, he eventually broke into the Co-op and stole the cash, hid out in the stunted tree growth between the pond and the marsh, slept in a culvert where we brought him food just after dark for three days till he was gone and was never mentioned again except by the cops who questioned a few of us; Harold, a large soft boy without a father so we felt a bond, though his father was dead, a Seventh Day Adventist unable to attend movies or watch TV and attending church on Saturday, he was odd but no worse than the rest of us . .
he once made a camera and developed his own photographs, blurred, grainy ghost images of us in groups, of Joey's horse, of the mine splintered against the bleached light of sky, and I think he became a cop when he grew up; Penny, Dougie Miller, Walter Miller, I knew little about, except they were all bullies and admired other bullies, were all large, athletic and might have seemed fit to succeed in their harsh world but had their own

damage which lurked behind the eyes — Penny perhaps the worst of all, not just a bully but a sick boy edging toward adult evil, was decapitated by a runaway coal cart not long after he went to work in the pit. Others, many others I came to know slightly as names attached to the staring faces of the circle of children watching on that first morning as we carried our belongings from the truck to the house.

* * *

"Your father is . . ."
"Shut up, Wayne!"
". . . a jailbird . . . jail . . . jail . . . jail . . . BIRD . . ."
"Fuck off Wayne!" He eluded me running to the screen door of my house where my mother was visible inside standing at the stove, her back to us.
"Mrs. MacNeil, Jackie told me to fuck off."
My mother turned and stared at him.
"Why don't you then, Wayne."

* * *

The feverish games of spring, the head seared by the excited rebirth of movement, the feet squelching heavily across the still wet ground and pant legs sucking water up to the knees.
Argument. Pure glittering spheres of glass flicked across beaten clay. Knees stained, chill against the steaming earth while your back soaks up the sun heat till you boldly fling aside jackets and sweaters to feel the breeze puffing, cooling, through your damp shirt. Spirit expanding.
Staring at the sun through the prismatic flaws of a glass marble. Toward the infinite.

* * *

When he returned I would tell him how I picked coal, dragging the seventy-five pound bags home to fuel the fire, only selling an occasional bag to get money for myself; how I'd saved all year to buy a telescope after I'd bought a small book with colored illustrations explaining astronomy; how I'd taught myself to swim (fear, a green translucency, pulling me down); how Penny had stopped me on the tracks before I even knew who he was and told me he would pound my face the next time he saw me so when I saw him a few days later, his back to me as I came out of the dim interior of the Co-op, I struck the back of his head with a can of beans, knocking him to the ground, and ran home in terror but finding later my bizzare act of violence had won a confused admiration. ("Yeah the skinny one . . . he's nuts, let him alone.") How I tied a rope to the ruin of World War II fortifications and hung a few feet below the edge of the thirty foot cliff to dig out coal from an exposed seam, then bagged it among the tumbled rocks below and dragged it to the cliff top and half a mile to home, (when he returned I imagined we would do this together, gathering tons of coal with him to carry the leaden sacks); how I'd learned to shoot the 30-30, which Joey would sneak from his brother's room, tracking the gulls till they were far out over the dazzling water, suddenly folding up like a piece of wind blown paper and vanishing in the distant impact . . .

He sent me a Christmas card he'd drawn himself of an old-fashioned car, the puffs of exhaust holding the letters MERRY CHRISTMAS.

* * *

"When Daddy comes home we'll move away from here."

Mattie, John, and Ann nod over their soup.

"I don't want to."

"Jack? Well dear . . . I know you've made friends here but you'll make new friends somewhere else . . . somewhere nice." My mother offers understanding but fear lights her eyes too.

"I don't want to move again."

"But why Jack?"

"I don't know."

* * *

Joey's father, George Sullivan, sitting in a rocking chair in the huge porch, once a summer kitchen before the old stove came, and now housing the coal for the fireplace and even a stall for the great sway-backed horse when the rotting barn got too cold. He sat rocking, smoking a pipe and staring at a bucket half full of water whose surface was regularly ringed by a plop of water leaking through the roof.

"Da!" Joey spoke to him as we came in, water running from us. Mr. Sullvan kept his eyes fixed on the bucket, jotting down a figure in a notebook and waving us away with his pipe.

Mrs. Sullivan, always in the overheated kitchen, huge billowing figure beneath flowered tents of cotton, the smells of cooking always about her even when she put on the black cloth coat to go to town with one of the older boys. Outside she always looked strangely diminished, a short stocky figure wrestling herself onto the seat of the dark green Ford. She would hang our wet clothes near the stove and make us tea and chips.

"What's Da doing?"

This time he was figuring out the weight of a drop of water. His method was to weigh a bucket, then count how many drops were needed to fill it, weigh it again and divide this figure less the bucket weight by the number of drops. I can smile now at this method but his curiosity still seems the essence of science. He wondered about everything and set about, with a total lack of formal education, unraveling these individual mysteries, naively creating a world in reverse. He was laughed at by nearly everyone, though it wasn't possible to dislike him, until someone realized one of his projects had been the keeping of a daily weather diary over nearly fifty years in this one location and he eventually sold all the diaries to the meteorological service for several thousand dollars.

Joey and I sat idly talking one afternoon after we'd been out with the rifle. Mr. Sullivan sat at the far end of the battered parlour carving a figure from a block of wood, his bent aquiline face mimicking two stuffed seagulls (taxidermy another skill he'd taught himself) who seemed to peer over his shoulder from their perch atop the upright piano.

Joey cocked the rifle aiming it at various objects in the room. Mr. Sullivan would know Joey wasn't allowed to handle the rifle but it was never his way to mention anything of this nature. Only his wife disciplined or kept any semblance of order but she was uptown today in the company of the owner of the 30-30. Joey drew a bead on the large wooden radio on the mantle where the bass notes of "Wake Up Little Susie" were rattling the old set against the dulled mirror hanging there. He pulled the trigger.

The whole room seemed to explode over my head, even the words of the song scattered falling shards along with the wood, glass, metal and plaster.

Mr. Sullivan didn't even look up. "Lazy bastard," he muttered, "Won't even get off his arse to shut off a radio."

* * *

When he came home I went everywhere with him. I waited in the car when he went to job interviews, did the shopping with him and went along when he looked up old acquaintances who might help him. Everything was a source of wonder . . . the car . . . I had pictured him walking home along the tracks I travelled nearly every day, but he drove right into the yard and was at the door before we even had a warning, a suitcase in one hand and a bottle jutting out of a jacket pocket. We were all over him, except Ann who was so young he might have been a stranger, but then we were all shy, standing dumbly near my mother and answering his questions with a no, or a yes. After a while he gave each of us some money and Mom asked me to take Mattie, Ann and John to the store and maybe for a walk around the shore.

Then they were alone in the house.

I went everywhere with him and I went into many places even going to meet the mountie to whom he reported for his parole, but sometimes he went to a bootlegger's (he wasn't allowed to drink on parole so he avoided the taverns, with me anyway) and the bootlegger wouldn't let me come in, though others did, so I had to stay in the car. I had done this as long as I could remember. He would go into a tavern when we were out and I would be given money to go to a store, then I'd sit in the car for an hour or two waiting for him. I would do this when I was four, from then on. It made my mother angry so I never mentioned it and anyway she didn't understand that I enjoyed it, that it made me closer to my father, being responsible for myself and giving him this minor gift of freedom. But I hadn't done it in a long time. I didn't want to spend money on candy and pop, there was nothing in this strange neighborhood for me to do,   so I sat in the car until the hot dusty stink of an old car on a summer day began to make me feel sick. I walked a numbing circuit of the yard. I could have gone to the house and asked for him but it seemed too embarrassing.

What would he think? It occurred to me I could walk home from there but he had left the keys in the car and I agonized over that for a while till I thought to put them in the glove compartment where I was sure he'd think to look.

I ran home with an incredible feeling of release.

I was already in bed when he came home in a taxi to confess my loss and the disappearance of the keys. My mother was laughing even though he began to sound angry. She explained what had happened. "That's the last time he'll ever come with me!" he yelled and my shame seemed to blaze up in the dark of my room but I fell asleep repeating my mother's reply, "He's almost grown up and starting to think for himself."

* * *

It was bad for them in ways I knew nothing of. They argued and we were sent outside in the day and to bed at night. He drank more and stayed away and they were angry at each other and at us and yet there was still more joy in all of us. We'd been saved from something and lost to something else and none of us, least of all four children aged three to ten understood what this meant.

Then my father came home one evening drunker than I'd seen him and my mother rolled out the hide-a-way bed, glancing at me every so often where I sat watching the television after the others were in bed. He fell asleep over his cold late supper and she woke him and helped him to the bed and began undressing him but something sent him into a rage in which he was shouting one moment, nearly crying the next and my mother all the while trying to reason and soothe, till she seemed to break and suddenly was yelling and crying too, one alternating with the other. It looked to me if they would just cry at the same time it would all be washed away, but then I just stared at the blurred television image unable to move and wishing they'd send me to bed.

Then he had stood up and struck her. She cursed him and it seemed an impossible thing coming from her. I didn't move until he'd struck her again and she fell back. I was on his back suddenly, my hands clawing at him, inadequate fists finding their mark while I screamed, "I hate you . . . I hate you . . ." for what seemed a long time while my mother pulled at us and I couldn't tell if she was trying to help me or trying to pull me off. Finally he flung us both aside, pulled on a few scattered pieces of clothing and was gone toward the kitchen.

I lay half on, half off the bed. My mother righted a chair and sat down, staring blankly, not crying anymore. My eyes kept wandering stupidly to the TV screen while I listened to the car start up, drive from the yard and up the road, receding almost to stuttering silence, then stopping and returning. The lights swept the room, fluttered over my mother and me where we sat dumbly and listened as the engine stopped, the car door slammed, then the kitchen door.

He came into the room and sat dejectedly on the edge of the bed tugging at his clothing. She went over to him and took up where she'd left off, what seemed so long ago, undressing him. When he was lying down, the blankets tucked up around his chest, she left the room. I was sensing all this, my eyes completely averted while they went through this without once referring to me but when my mother had gone from the room my father suddenly sat up, his head hanging in a broken way and said, "So you hate me, boy."

"No." I lied, for at that moment a limitless rage and hate rose up in me. Simultaneously an impossible sorrow snuffed out this hatred and after a moment of numbness I found I could speak haltingly, "No . . . I don't." My voice was almost a whisper and I got up, finally able to move and walked from the room without looking at him and began to climb the stairs in darkness while a feeling of relief grew in me with each upward step. When I reached the hall upstairs I heard his voice clear and steady, "Good night, son."

Ray Smith / Mabou

Ray Smith was born at Inverness in 1941 and did much of his growing up in and around Mabou. He attended Dalhousie University and in 1969 published **Cape Breton is the Thought Control Centre of Canada,** a radically unconventional work of fiction. His second book, **Lord Nelson Tavern,** appeared in 1974. A reviewer for MacLean's suggests Smith is "Something rare in Canadian writing — a genuine absurdist."

He worked briefly as a systems analyst and has been a teacher in Montreal since 1971.

> *The summers were sunnier then, says the sentimental imagination looking back to childhood, but I'm not terribly sentimental about the summers I remember. I have tried, these many years, not to be so. But the fact is, I spent the summers of my childhood and my youth in Mabou and, whatever the weather was really like, the memories are golden; and at the center of me now, wherever I go, no matter how I feel, there is a golden memory of childhood shimmering. "When, in disgrace with Fortune and men's eyes," when alone or afraid, when gazing upon ugliness in this world; or when enjoying the civilized languor of a pastis on the Champs Elysee, a pint of the best bitter at a local pub in Chelsea, the gezelligheid of a family bar in Holland; or when skiing the mountain powder of Switzerland, Austria or Colorado; when watching a sunrise over the south Pacific from a Qantas 747 or a sunset along the length of Sydney Harbour (in Australia);   in happiness or despair . . . I never forget that I was a little boy in paradise, among the trees and hills and ocean waves of Mabou; the laughter and music and warmth of Mabou; and maybe, if I work hard, and live a good life, and I'm lucky . . . then perhaps I'll get to live in paradise again someday.*

The Dwarf in his Valley Ate Codfish

by Ray Smith

1. *The Great Man*

Long noses and petulance; the Great Man himself used to sit here, but that was in the old days when things were not as they are now. Is it a sense of loss we feel? Yes, I believe so, for we are weak. I do not like a south wind blowing.

There are many things to forget. See, here, carved into the doorstep: 'M.E.' Neat lettering, deep, straight and with every serif in fine proportion, to commemorate the night the buffalo passed by, surly and awesome, a shadow and a rumble. *You remember!*

Make a vista for yourself; I will not disturb it; I am going round to the back of the house to the trees. Come if you wish, or not as also you wish. I will not trouble you.

I'm glad; one worries about proportion.

I have always wanted power; I begin to fear I have not got it in me. Oh yes, at times, under some circumstances, but always artificial. We ponder the fate of the codwife and her dark love...

Remember this shed from back over the (so many!) years. It was in there that we played the rumple game. How did it go? Yes. After all, what else can you do with a daffodil? You have a sleek sense of humour, sliding otter jokes that end with a splash. Ah! The tyranny of delight!

I see horses, one flesh coloured, one lime green, two red and two orange and the second orange one is leaping over a lime green sawhorse. It has not moved in six years. Beyond that (beyond the six years) I cannot (would not) vouch for it. Perhaps the Great Man... but that is no matter. Not *now*.

Was Alexander the Great's horse called Bucephalus? I have a feeling he was. History lacks sincerity; so I have always thought. The Great Man once accused history of three crimes, none of which was committed in the name of passion. The magistrate tossed the case out of court for lack of evidence. This tree will mean something to you . . .

Curious, doubtless, I never knew. But then, there is so much one never knows. Don't you find that so? I once saw a falcon and thought myself lucky. If you enquire into the history of playing cards you will find, I surmise, that the Queen of Spades has always been evil . . .

Uptopian characters always play a local variation of chess, inferior because of the writer's blind spots. But think! Think of the wildman or the fascinating mystery of Basilisk-Thorpe at Arras in '93. But then, even I sing at times for no reason at all. Yes.

Save string.

Fatuity is excusable for the same reason that sincerity is insufferable; it all depends upon the bending of the reeds when, under the scudding clouds, the wind comes in over the marshes, nervous, chill, aged . . .

The long grass . . . I once thought happiness was balanced tension but the nostrum is no longer of much use to me. That does not make it less true—you'll recall the crow and the rune.

Have a lemon . . . go ahead. No lemon groves o'erhang the hoary Don. Did you know (you who have loved a red-haired girl) that the shell (of the oyster) is still around; I think it is in one of those cupboards you browse through on a rainy day. Old books, chocolate boxes full of trinkets, etc.

Red and blue stripes: that is the key.

Say something.

Plantagenet.

Codfish.

Nettles.

There's a political pun to be made out of Caesar's crossing the Rubicon; I can't be bothered explaining it for it is complicated and, I expect, of little interest to any but me.

Fol-de-ree

Fol-de-ray

Turn a key

End the day.

One sometimes wonders about dimensions. He did, frequently.. mused upon the difference between weight and specific gravity.... made several cunning observations. Or: consider a planet. Yes, exactly, the Great Man said as much himself numerous times.

He looked into the alcove (the buffalo again) and thought to himself: any God worth a damn would surely have the sense of humour to put up real red, white and blue striped north and south poles. Well, he said, really, I don't think it's too much to ask, after all, he said, the aged pederast once . . .

Thus (or so) the Aged Pederast:

An old room, very old, with small sooty windows, old *objets d'art* from years past (why the past itself!) cluttered about. The fireplace doesn't draw well. In his worn chair sits the aged pederast reading a pornographic book. The pederast is snickering; he wipes the saliva from his chin with a dirty, hardened handkerchief . . . We steal closer . . .

Possibly. I'm not sure.

What is it about marzipan? There's something about marzipan. You can't trust people with pens.

'France, Spain, Italy, Germany, Poland, Russia, Sweden, Turkey,/ Arabia, Palestine, Persia, Hindustan, China, Tartary, Siberia,/ —the feet upon the endless stair— 'Egypt, Lybia, Ethiopia, Guinea, Caffraria, Negroland, Morocco,/ Congo, Zaara, Canada, Greenland, Carolina, Mexico,/ Peru, Patagonia, Amazonia, Brazil: . . .' You quote from the bard.

Have a handkerchief, his nose is running.

Wouldn't it be great, she thought, to be a walrus! (I have a friend who is happy much of the time.)

No, not you, of course . . . We wonder what to do about the Beautiful and so we draw maps showing holes in the ground; but when we try to use the maps the holes have unaccountably moved. Holes do that.

See . . . there . . . a man on crutches.

Now the Great Man used to be brought out here in the evenings to . . . listen I suppose. He was blind as a bat by then, but the ears of a bat too. The women used to say it was so touching, but women always say that sort of thing. See, here is the trailing arbutus; it was his favourite flower for some reason unknown to the rest of them. Here, have a collander. No, really, I have a whole carton in my room.

Yes, all right. Perhaps we could wear sweaters as I know your dislike for clouds which assume the shape of earthly objects.

I beg your pardon?

Possibly; in any case, I'm off to the beach now. Think upon the broken pillar and the goatherd's jolly song.

Harrooo . . . .

II. Gladys

Gladys: but then she never knew the difference. You wonder sometimes, you really wonder how long, how long O! Israel. You can try erasing but the whole web is ersatz. It's like trying to extract minutes from yesterdays. She had style; she also had long hair. The hair probably explained more. I don't know.

'So,' he said and walked down the mountain. What the hell can you do, he asked himself, what can anyone do about panoramas? He just walked down the mountain until he came to a tavern and he went into the tavern and got drunk. No one cared. They didn't even ask him for money. You don't care, he yelled, you don't give a damn. What the hell do I have to do, expose myself? (It was one of those countries.)

So he exposed himself and no one gave a damn.

Gladys! Gladys! he cried and they turned away. Out in the street his feet tended naturally on down the mountain. God knows what happened to him after that. Perhaps we'll find out later. I wasn't there at the time, but I heard it from someone or other. It is substantially true.

You were sitting at the far end of the long table (so elegant) and I could hardly see you because the candles were the only light in the room and you said to me, 'Marjorie, this is the damndest best bouillabaisse I've ever tasted,' and I thought about it not having *racasse*, which you can't get here. When *was* that? I remember the glitter; there was at least as much inside me. But I don't know; what are you supposed to say about crimes of this sort? Are they really crimes? Perhaps that's more to the point. We talk about Macedonian blood fueds that were ageless when Alexander the Great was counting his fingers for Aristotle, we talk about wergeld and we can go to an art gallery and see paintings worth a king's ransom. So.

Take for example a fellow I knew in the army. Mashie-Niblick was his name. An officer and a gentleman, a really despicable piece of humanity. He got himself cashiered for gambling debts and, having learned his role well from a lot of chintzy pot-boilers, never got back up again. Finally hung himself from a sconce by his regimental tie. It was pretty silly, really, he was eighty seven at the time. I believe he was afraid of lightning.

In any case, this is the lino print block. I suppose it should have been destroyed but my wife restrains me. He listened to the radio a lot while Gladys was still alive and she thought he was in love with me. 'Marjorie,' she would say, 'he has to be in love with you, you're so much more beautiful.' Although I wasn't really, just more photogenic. Gladys could never see the difference. I mean, she never wore a girdle and I think men adored her for that. I tried not wearing one but it just didn't work. I have these solid child-bearing hips. It was the same even when I was young enough that it mattered. In any case here is, as I said, the lino print block.

Gladys, Gladys: I always loved her, I always feel that when she dies the world will end. It was cool and bright the morning he set out. The only sounds were birdsong and the rustling of the dew. Clear, so clear! and bright. He sang a song as he walked along and the song he sang was 'The Bottom Rung.' (And ring it did . . . later.) There's nothing like beginning a journey; we've all done it. It was a shame his ended so quickly and so tragically. Ten girls in the county swore they never would marry and at least one, the ugliest and stupidest, was able to keep her threat. Revelation is the bread of fools, the bane of merchants and the salve of kings. So much for bloody journeys.

Take this street, for instance. Fifty years ago it was nothing but a quaggy swamp. Progress, they say, marches on. But when you're my age you find your mind back in that swamp. The swamp harboured wildfowl, doubtless, and there were sedges of one sort and another. The world should make a place for bogs. Yes, I mean that, in spite of what happened to Gladys. You see, in spite of it all, she wasn't too bright. Midnight wanderings: well really, now, what can you expect?

Once I was sitting in a bleak tavern. It was the wrong time of day and the only other person there (besides the arthritic barmaid who appeared every now and then) was a rather dispirited prostitute doing a crossword puzzle. She had propositioned me earlier in a sadly apologetic way and I had thanked her, apologetically no. We chatted a bit about the weather while she chipped away at her memory. Then she asked me for a six letter word for 'yoke' beginning with 'z'. I said, 'Zeugma,' and she said, no, it wasn't a Polish crossword. We got it worked out after a while. The funny thing—macabre if you wish—was that it was in this very tavern that Gladys had first met Stanislaus Zeugma, her—shall we say?—fate . . .

Or, see that fellow just going into that house across the street . . yes . . . well, he wears a chastity belt . . . yes, voluntarily . . . and his wife is a prostitute too. It's all over the place but it's keeping me alive because it's milled from washed wheat.

She liked gambling a lot and was rather good at it. So it was with some misgivings that I heard them ask her, 'Hey Margie, how about a game of strip poker?' There were six men and just her and when the game was over she was fully clothed. After she had teased us a bit she took off too. She was always a good sport which is why, I think, everyone disliked her so much. She disliked artichokes.

I remember Gladys at school; she was the cause of much violence. Old Nosey's life was ruined by the scandal. It was then we saw she was utterly amoral. Doorways meant nothing to her. It's infuriating, you see; you work and work building something and at the very last minute you find out you've used water instead of glue. (You wonder what happened to the glue and then you brush your teeth . . .) Oh yes, she had a way about her. If only she hadn't giggled so much.

"Why?' he yelled when he had emerged from the sewer, 'Why?'

'Who wants to know?' they called back.

'A wayfaring stranger.'

'Screw strangers.'

And so. Usually they were an hospitable bunch but you'd be unwise to depend on it. Oh, he stumbled about, muttering, trying as we all do to find a dignified out, but all he came up with was Gladys's name. So he took another swig from his bottle and cried, 'Gladys . . . Gladys!' As he should have expected, they tore him apart and fed him to the dogs. That was the sort of effect she had on people. The morning the duel was to be fought she said to me, 'Margie, I deserve this, don't I?' and I replied, 'Gladys, you sure do.' It seemed to make her happy; God knows, she needed happiness.

III. The Shadow People

I remember the one with the artificial breasts saying how deep do you have to go anyway? Isn't there a limit? I mean . . . She crossed her legs so that her skirt rode up, the exposure giving her as much pleasure as it gave us. The secret, she once told Madelaine, is an aura of prurience. Along with her perfume she wore some secret scent with aphrodisiacal qualities. We found out later it was a drop of fish oil.

It just goes on. The frightening part of it is that nothing gets added, but things die and get taken away until there's nothing left but the going on. Process is horrible. But there are still hedgehogs. Remember the hedgehog; consider the hedgehog; venerate the hedgehog. So also:

Codfish

Cauliflowers

And Mira the Wonderful.

Here, you can't do that . . . Really, though, in a place like this we'll have no stories about altarboys and streetlights. I've heard them all anyway. Try one about the raven.

Take the Marianas Trench, for e.g.; you can't go a hell of a lot deeper than that. Or in people, is the sole or the soul the deeper? or the gut? Or how many fish live deeper than the sole, as if that solved anything. What a lot of nonsense; there's nothing more meaningless than connections.

That far under the water there was no light and he found himself feeling his way along the stainless steel wall, his fingers probing for a break, a turning. It was not much after that his bro - ther found a moosehead in the piano and an unnamed girl, dressed in white, looked up and down the street before stepping into a dark doorway. It went on like that day after day until the old man died. His last request was for a kipper and when they said he shouldn't eat kippers in his condition he bawled at them 'Not to eat, you fools, to look at. Bah!' And so expired.

The question he was putting to them was this: Why can't it

all happen on a seashore? You have your eel-grass, your driftwood, waves, sea urchins, rocks, wind, sky, weather, sea . . . Hell, what else is there? Run it up over a dune and add some sex and there you are. To hell with formalizations; to hell with inlaid ceilings and pillars; what the hell do they matter? He was a brash young fellow, they said, and you know what they're like. J.D. (going under the name of A.C.) once told the feeble crow to go castigate the rood. People listened to him, though, because whatever he said had the heft of an anvil.

Once she got mixed up with a shoe salesman who read Blake. He had a great mind, that shoe salesman, really, just great. Some people would have said great in the sense of fat-headed but that was all they knew. Things can be learned from driving rods into the ground, but nowadays they use explosives and that's taken all the fun out of it, all the mystery. She thought the seismograph was a device used by charlatan mind readers. The last we had heard of her she had eloped with the gimpy alchemist and his retarded assistant. Presumably he changed her.

Once they tried to do fireflies; sat around a meadow one night, friendly at first then silent, then snarling at each other. Oh, the fireflies came all right, but never enough at once and they could never anticipate a blink. After that they pretty well stuck to artificial flowers. Once they went to Stonehenge and came back with the flu. But they could work together and every man Jack of 'em had a taste for endive. They hung together . . . just like pirates. *You* know.

Chessmen and the far-off lights; things like that drove her crazy after a while. He knew it was coming, he had seen it from very early on. When she had been gone three months, he went too. The memory of them is sharp but it is only a few pictures and the colour is too bright for truth. It's like a one-eyed man catching a ball: lunge at truth and you get a broken nose. (At least that was what he said, but neither he nor his father much believed in the epigrams they both rolled out so easily. 'Epigrams are like doughnuts,' the father wrote from Burma. 'They got holes in the middle.') Everyone pretended to believe it. They were very understanding; and very loathsome.

So the time passed and passes. One wonders how long it can go on. It's the happiness that goes first, and it matters damn little what goes after that. We pick up daisies and dream of train rides. Hate sneaks in like juice into a grapefruit. One day it leaps out at your eye. Something will snap somewhere. Somehow it will get at them sooner or later, the Great Man, Gladys and The Shadow People. Until then: long noses and petulance.